# The Longest Pregnancy

by *Melissa*

*Melissa Fraterrigo*

Swallow's Tale Press
at The University of West Alabama

Copyright © 2006 Melissa Fraterrigo
All rights reserved, including electronic text
ISBN 0-930501-27-6, hardback
ISBN 0-930501-26-8, trade paper
isbn 13 978-0930501-26-6, trade paper
isbn 13 978-0930501-27-3, hardback
Library of Congress Control Number 2005938295

Printed on acid-free paper.
Printed in the United States of America,
Publishers Graphics
Hardcover binding by: Heckman Bindery
Typesetting and page layout: Joe Taylor
Proofreading: Margaret Walburn, Tricia Taylor,
Angela Brown, Alexius White, Joel Bonner, Liza Pugh

Cover design: Joe Taylor
Cover Layout: Joe Taylor
Cover art: Bruce New
Cover photo of ugly tart: Tina Jones

Many of these stories have also appeared elsewhere, in slightly different forms: "The Shark Swimmers" in *Arts & Letters*, "The Attached Couple" in *The Massachusetts Review*, "Scar Serum" in *Other Voices*, "Memory Woman" in *South Dakota Review*, "Madera Bree" in *Confrontation*, "The Longest Pregnancy" in *Carolina Quarterly*, "The Hunted" in *Black Ridge Review*, "The Country of Women" in *So to Speak*, "Bejeweled" in *The Emerging Writers' Network*, and "The Strongest Woman in the World" in *Notre Dame Review*.

*Acknowledgements:* I am deeply grateful to Rachael Perry, Alicia Conroy, Donna Sparkman, Anthony Doerr, and George Looney for reading these stories. Your thoughtful insight, careful criticism, and support have made this collection stronger. Thanks to Wendell Mayo who taught me that everything in fiction is possible and Bonnie Jo Campbell who showed me the way. This book was conceived through the initial generosity of Penn State Altoona with special gratitude to Dinty Moore. Many thanks to my family: Carl and Judy Fraterrigo, my brother Chris and my sister Jennifer — best friend and reader— who have all in their way both supported and inspired me. Finally, Peter Seymour has offered me more than I could ever imagine through the strength of his love.

Livingston Press is part of The University of West Alabama,
and thereby has non-profit status.
Donations are tax-deductible:
brothers and sisters, we need 'em.

first edition
6 5 4 3 3 2 1

# Table of Contents

*For Pete*

*With thanks, also*
*To Erica, Michelle, and Sarah*

# The Longest Pregnancy

# The Shark Swimmers

*T*o us, they will always be the family that swims with sharks. They will shuffle around with sun-bleached hair and bronze skin, rough knees and elbows from years of submersion in salty waters. They will continue to receive discounts at the Food Lion where their grandparents and great-grandparents shopped before there even was a shark show. Around town, people will recall a time when the apartments along Torrence Avenue were freshly painted and nearly every storefront displayed a tiny rubber shark.

Though it's been years since the tourists visited our town, the red awnings that line the beach still stand. Now the boardwalk creaks in the faintest of winds and Saturday afternoons pass without interruption. We spend days at home mowing our lawns, complaining to our wives, feeling the weight of regret circle our knees.

The shark swimmers' shows were once a common weekend activity. Before each show, small, dark men in caps released the sharks from their pens. The sharks sped through the water, streamlined bodies thrashing the waves. The shark swimmers trained the sharks from the moment they first lured them to the southeastern shore. During noon feedings, when we weren't in school, we watched the men toss chunks of tuna or dolphin to the sharks, their upper jaws snapping forward over vicious points of teeth. We jumped, bumped against each other. The four of us were like that—always together. We had been classmates since the first grade and we thought we knew everything about each other's lives.

Our fathers worked nights at L&M Glass, standing for eight- and nine-hour shifts, operating hydraulic machines or mechanical cutters. They walked to work each afternoon while our mothers made casseroles. We spent our time buying Cokes and bags of barbecue chips. Sometimes we talked about girls, although there was only one that interested us.

One of the swimmers, Mariona, attended our school, yet we never approached her alone and out of water. She was redheaded, the oldest child, and anytime we waved to her family she scooped her face behind her hand, annoyed to be the object of our looks. We admired the shark swimmers. Each of them could seize the fin of a great white with bare hands and the shark would pull them for a few moments before they had to let go.

They were all fast swimmers. They spun through the water, their hands breaking waves like steely torpedoes—but that's not to say that their act was without injury. Not even they were exempt from misery. No one talks about the baby, the almost swimmer, but everyone remembers how sad we were that day. We still can't help but think it never should have happened, how she might have changed everything for Mariona, for Brad—for all of us.

Mariona had interests beyond water; she dreamed of a life on land. Instead of flip-flops, she yearned for leather shoes that covered her toes. It was the job running the fortune-teller booth on the boardwalk she desired. Mariona could determine if a person would live a life of fortitude or heartache. Maybe she saw into her own future. It's easy to say that all the steps leading up to Mariona's last swim were for some indistinguishable destiny, some truthful moment. Even now, we can't be sure. Right up until her last swim she practiced with her family every day after school. She completed weight training alongside her father, stretched thick rubber bands between her hands, built triceps and biceps to rival any member of the school softball team. She ran miles on the beach between her parents, sweat dotting her forehead, flushing her cheeks in such a lovely way. The family couldn't exist without Mariona. She was the one, quiet and demure, who everyone came to see. She filled the bleachers. The showcase, the headliner. The beautiful girl who swam with sharks.

Unlike her shark-swimming parents, Mariona had skin that remained white despite months spent in the blazing sun. She reminded us of one of the *Cosmo* cover girls, the way she poised her head, looked at us in the bleachers without ever really seeing us. The suit she wore accented the slim curve of her neck. It skimmed the lines of her body like the wake the sharks made as they sped through the surf. The black fabric contrasted her skin, which became a pale trace in the water until it looked as if she might fade away before our very eyes. One time, she nearly did. They were banking on her at seventeen. She had become the headliner almost overnight. Each of the shark swimmers participated in the show, but as her parents grew older, the responsibility shifted to Mariona to perform the bulk of the spectacular acts that sold tickets.

Mariona's mother's looks had begun to ebb. And along with her looks she had lost much of her original speed. She could still catch hold of the shark's dorsal fin, but it was more difficult for her to hang on. So with age, she took to smaller tricks, being towed behind two scalloped hammerheads, or trained the baby tiger sharks to swim in polygons, rhombi, and geometrical figures. Mariona's father, a strong, stout man of fifty, did most of the balancing acts.

He held Mariona on his shoulders while balancing on the ski board, racing the sharks in the section of waters roped off in 25-meter lanes. Previously, he always won.

On Saturdays we used the money we'd saved from edging lawns and bagging groceries to attend the shark show. Mariona was the one we came to see. She glided alongside the sharks and the great white would let her fix her hands over its retractable eyes. We were there the first time she performed what the papers called a miraculous feat. Mariona revealed afterward in a rare newspaper interview that it was the first time she'd attempted to lift herself on top of the shark's tubular body.

Once on top of the shark, she positioned her arms for balance, placed her feet in a plié, and bent her knees. She rode the shark up and down the coast to our heroic yelps and cheers. Minutes after she jumped off the shark, Mariona stood on the dock alongside her parents. Her mouth was twisted and we weren't sure if she was grinning at the wonderment of it all or if the sun merely glinted off the water's surface and into her eyes.

When we closed our eyes at night it was Mariona that we saw. She flew across water, anticipating the twisted motion of the giant fish, hair whipping behind her, trim hips swaying as they tunneled through waves. Although we didn't have girlfriends, we imagined that someday, somehow, Mariona would be ours.

One night, we saw Mariona at the boardwalk standing outside the fortune teller's booth. It was the first time she spoke directly to us. We were waiting to have our futures read by the woman in a gold cape. "I can tell you your fortunes," said Mariona, shocking us with her lilting voice. "For free." If it were anyone other than Mariona, we probably wouldn't have followed her to a bench in front of the bumper cars where she instructed us to sit down. She told us to turn our arms toward her so she could read our veins, which she called avenues of destiny. The candied lights from the Ferris wheel shimmered in her fiery mane. Brad went first. "A beautiful woman will fall in love with you," said Mariona.

"Does that mean you want to grab a burger with me?"

We couldn't believe Brad—how could he think he had a right to demand anything of Mariona?

"I only tell you what I see."

Brad had more questions. His voice pitched and rocked forward. "Well, look again." He pushed his arms up beneath her chin. Mariona's lips firmed. She didn't move. The breeze flipped up the ends of her hair. "You know so much—tell me," said Brad.

Mariona turned her head, stepped in front of Tim Manzeti. His parents were in the process of divorcing, and Tim was barely coping. "Your mother will have a change of heart. She will forgive your father's infidelity," said Mariona before moving on to another of us. Tim thanked her, even bowed, kept nodding his head.

When Derrick opened his arms toward Mariona, she looked up at him. "You are going to invent a new type of car."

"Is that true?" we asked.

"Sure." She didn't wait for a response.

"Come on, let's blow this joint," said Brad. He reached out, grabbed Mariona's fingers.

"Don't touch me," spat Mariona. "Not with what those hands will touch." She turned on her heels and strode off.

"What's with her?" asked Brad.

We watched her tall form blend in with the crowd. Tim ran after her, tried to ask when his mom would change her mind about the divorce, but Mariona refused to pay him any attention.

Days after Tim Manzeti had his fortune read, he paraded around school. He completed all his homework, turned in an extra credit report on the Battle of the Bulge for American history and volunteered to gather canned goods for the food bank drive. Every day we asked him if he'd heard anything about the divorce. When he told us the divorce papers had been put away and that his parents had decided to remain together we became Mariona's greatest fans, even making M's in the air when we saw each other.

We wanted to approach her, ask her to go toOogies with us for a basket of fries or press her for more details about our futures, although we couldn't make those kinds of demands on her. On Saturdays, though, we were able to watch her glide over choppy waves, standing on the back of the shark with its massive gills and pinpoint eyes. Mariona never flinched. The shark darted through the water, always ready to toss her off into the jumbled surf.

At that time we didn't realize how dissatisfied Mariona was with her life. Dana Reynolds told us later at our high school reunion that Mariona had taken to drawing hearts all over her binders in chemistry, where they were lab partners. Mariona seldom looked up from her artistry, and she never took notes. She'd fill in boxes on multiple-choice exams at random and still ace tests. "She would line the outside of the heart with a thick band, or add lacy trimmings. She always added M + J. One day she caught me looking at her drawings," said Dana.

"Do you mind?" Mariona had asked, covering her work with a wrist.

"I was just thinking about your boyfriend," said Dana. "I don't think I've ever met him."

"That makes two of us."

"Freaky," Dana told us, shrugging her shoulders.

What did we really know about Mariona? We were more interested in what she could do for us. We began staying out at night when the boardwalk, usually a blur of reds and yellows, blended into the dark and the only illumination came from the streetlights.

We walked along the pier, popping our gum, passing Friar Tuck's Arcade, the corn dog cart, the Pizza Pantry with its oversized, dancing pink mouse. Tim said he could feel Mariona's presence. We didn't believe him in the least, until we turned at the bumper cars and saw her perched on the guardrail of the kiddie sailboat rides. We stopped, our clothes suddenly feeling as if they belonged to someone else.

Brad spoke up. "Hey."

Mariona smiled at us, jumped down from the railing. She smelled like the sea and held her hands out for our arms. We circled around her, eager to hear more about our futures. Derrick went first. "All that reading will pay off in law school," said Mariona.

"Wow," said Derrick, "I don't even know a lawyer."

Tim, the scrappiest of us, was instructed to start lifting weights; he discovered he'd be rewarded with a wrestling scholarship. He started making muscles, imitating the guys from *Sports Illustrated*. Derrick fake-punched him in the stomach and Tim flopped over, pretended to be in pain.

"What about me?" asked Brad. "When is that babe entering my life?"

"Listen to me." Mariona grabbed the neck of Brad's T-shirt.

"What?!" Brad held his arms out.

"Just listen. When she approaches you, don't do it. You're going to mess everything up."

"Huh? Who? My lady?" By this time Mariona had tired of us. She let go of Brad's shirt and tucked her own into the waist of her shorts.

"If I told you everything it would change," said Mariona. "Trust me."

We shivered. "Why don't you come with us?" asked Brad, his voice soft and low. We didn't have any plans except to pile into

Brad's Toyota, play cards in Tim's basement, and maybe look at copies of his father's *Playboy*. Mariona didn't respond. Instead, she strode off as if she were late for an appointment.

*I*t was during our junior year that Derrick determined Mariona had taken a boyfriend. He was positive that he saw Mariona with a man who worked one of the boardwalk games get into a green Buick with a bent fender. "They were walking real slow and she was so close to him they almost looked like one giant 'I' under the streetlights." We asked him if he heard what they were talking about. "I followed them a ways. They stopped at the corner of Sixth and Waveland. He kissed her forehead and then they went in different directions."

We all knew the man. He'd worked on the boardwalk for as long as we could remember, dressed in concert T-shirts and corduroys even during the hottest days of August. Surely Mariona could do better. Brad took it the hardest. "Damn her!"

Soon after, she began sloughing off during shows. Mariona would let go of the shark's fin too soon or kick her heels up when her father positioned her on top of his shoulders. Mariona slid off his back, plopped into the water while the sharks swam by in droves. One day a picture of Mariona appeared in the newspaper. In it, Mariona's arms are folded across her chest; she was unwilling to get into the water. In the photo, her father had both hands out to her, beseeching. Mariona's lips were placid, two steel rods. The headline read, "Mariona Shuns Act." Editorials disputed whether Mariona had the right to quit swimming. Brochures advertising the act stocked every rest stop within one hundred miles. Some said her parents were too lax and that she needed discipline; swimming was her family duty. Others said she should have the right to take a hiatus; she was born into swimming and at the age of eighteen she could choose to give it up.

*O*ne night we were heading back from a party when Brad excused himself, said he'd meet up with us later. "Where you off to?" we asked.

"Nowhere," he snapped.

It was Tim's idea to follow him. We took our time, hiding behind garbage cans and bushes, pulling on tree branches. We moved stealthily. We hid behind parked cars and found Brad whistling, pulling apart leaves, tossing their torn remnants over his shoulder. We followed him past the factories on the east side of town, where most of us lived, to the place where vacationers rented two-story homes. Brad cut through an alley and turned down a street devoid of cars. He walked up to a split-level with a crushed-shell driveway. From the shadows, we watched him walk around to the back of the house and whistle a warbler's cry. He made the call again, this time louder. A few moments later the back gate opened. Mariona's mother stepped out.

We couldn't believe our eyes. She wore a long gown that hung to the ankles. She scooped Brad into her arms and we watched him kiss her, his hands playing with the hem of her dress.

When had Brad met Mariona's mother? What about her husband? We were both shamed and impressed. We wanted to ask him a million questions, yet knew that we never would—this was a secret and we were now a part of it.

*S*everal weeks after Mariona quit swimming, her mother announced her own pregnancy. Maybe they sensed Mariona's plan to leave the show and put her swimsuit to rest. We can only speculate. We couldn't help but think of Brad and what we'd witnessed. We didn't talk about what we'd seen, although all of us thought about Brad once we heard Mariona's mother was expecting. It would be her mother's last child, no doubt, and the town was thrilled with the idea of watching the pregnant shark swimmer's metamorphosis.

From the beginning, they publicized the birth just as they had advertised Mariona's riding skills. It was decided Mariona's mother would birth the baby in the ocean, the youngest family member to swim alongside the sharks. In the newspaper they posted weekly updates on her pregnancy and printed pictures of the little one swimming inside her mother. Tickets to their shows began to sell for over forty dollars!

The focus shifted away from Mariona and her refusal to be a part of the act. Instead, she helped set up the Saturday morning shows, carrying fish in metal buckets, standing to the side in shorts and a T-shirt, watching the show like the rest of us.

*A*s Mariona's mother swelled and puffed, her cheeks became rosy and youthful. The town held a name-the-baby contest at Hotz Drugs. For one dollar, we took turns writing possible names for the future shark swimmer on pieces of paper. The shark swimmers promised to draw the name at random from the top ten entries and present the winner with a fifty-dollar gift certificate. We each entered two or three times. We suggested watery names like Aqualine and Conchetta, Sandra and Shell. Brad refused to participate. He said the whole idea of birthing a baby in the water was stupid. What about infidelity, we silently wondered. How stupid was that?

We heard afterward that Mariona had predicted it all, that she'd warned her parents of the baby's future weeks before the birth took place. Supposedly, when they didn't listen to her, Mariona wrote her parents letters and placed them beneath the blankets on each side of their bed. When her father eased into bed, his letter crackled, bent like an accordion, and in exhaustion, he scanned it briefly and tossed it aside. Her mother was already asleep, retiring to bed an hour earlier. Her letter had slid beneath her pillow. In her mother's letter, Mariona had sketched a stick figure of a boy kissing the matron shark swimmer. It didn't matter. Her parents didn't listen to her and as the weeks wore on, weariness developed around Mariona's eyes.

On the day of the birth, they induced the labor so it would coincide with the one o'clock show. We took our place in the bleachers, bought a program, and arranged our sunglasses. Brad had bet us seventy dollars that he, too, could swim with sharks. Ever since we'd witnessed him with Mariona's mother he acted as if he was better than us. "They're nothing special," he said. "Anyone can do it." We didn't agree; we adored their talent, the feats they could perform. But who knew when to take Brad seriously?

Mariona's mother was already in the water, back against the dock, arms propped on the ledge. She was wearing a bikini top we'd never before seen and her rounded belly just capped the water. Her features were scrunched in pain. We watched the rise of her breasts quicken with each breath. Her feet, attached to white buoys, rocked with each wave while the obstetrician bobbed beside her in his orange life vest.

The labor was quick. Mariona's mother tossed her head back, cried out once, then again. With the final push she gave a strong kick and the baby rushed out.

The men in caps released the sharks from their cages as planned. We craned our necks, thought we saw the baby in the doctor's hands, in the red cloud of blood. Brad stood up like the rest of us so he could see better. "Watch this," he told us, jumping out of the bleachers and running toward the water. Never had anyone but the trained swimmers entered the water with sharks. The audience shrieked. The couple sitting next to us grabbed hands. We held our breath, shoulders bumping against one another.

Brad began the sidestroke, his form a blur of white. We squinted, watched the waves splash over his head, his mouth just clearing the surface.

Meanwhile, the sharks thought Brad was part of the show. They circled him, tail fins poised. That's when Brad screamed and his head went under and any bet was called off.

At the same time, a few feet from Brad, the obstetrician had just cut the umbilical, when naturally, another contraction struck Mariona's mother. She kicked the water and pulled under the can-shaped buoys, and with the upswing, waves ricocheted, one of which surprised the doctor. He swallowed water, spurted and gasped for air, and the slick baby he was holding slipped from his wide, sturdy hands.

In the excitement, none of us in the audience knew what had occurred. It wasn't until Mariona dove into the waves and we recognized that same vigorous kick that we realized something else had gone wrong. Mariona's red hair was hidden behind a mass of foam and spray, whitecaps interrupting the uniform blue-green. She punched the water, her hips a trough under the surface and dragged a sputtering Brad to shore.

By the time she turned around and swam out to the dock, the doctor had recovered from his coughing fit. He must have told Mariona's parents that the baby girl thought she was a fish, swimming right out of his hands. She had never even taken a breath of air. The entire hospital staff splashed into the water in their beach clothes. We watched as Mariona and her father dove under the surface for long stretches. It didn't take long for Mariona to find the baby with her pearly white arms outstretched, her arched legs still, positioned for the crawl. Mariona scooped the youngest of the family of swimmers out from its slow descent, umbilical cord twisting behind her. We watched Mariona hold the baby over her head. Water glinted on her virgin skin and light tracings of red hair. She passed the baby over to the hospital staff huddled on the dock where they worked to resuscitate, much more equipped for birth on land than in water, they'd later admit.

Mariona treaded water with her father while her mother remained attached to the buoys. The sharks swam the perimeter of the dock, churning the now calm water, a trail of bubbles in their wake.

They were ready to begin the show.

Mariona spoke to her parents. "She was already dead."

Brad stood knee-deep in the water, watching the swimmers until security guards flanked him on either side, grabbing his upper arms and yanking him onto the sand. Brad's head hung. "It's not my fault!" he screamed.

Who was he hoping would hear him—Mariona? Her mother? Perhaps us.

In the weeks following the baby's burial, we were surprised to discover it wasn't the fault of the clumsy doctor, nor were we to blame for failing to stop Brad. The baby was a stillborn. Her autopsy report was published and reporters from Orlando and New York flung themselves upon our town. Specials were aired nightly about the risk involved with alternative birth. The obstetrician from Lakeview Hospital was criticized in a three-day series aired on Channel 13. Both of Mariona's parents kept on with the show, they said, as a tribute to the tragedy that had struck their family.

Brad was fined for obstructing the performance and was forbidden from attending future shows. We saw him at the boardwalk at night. He offered us cigarettes from his own pack, but only Derrick was brave enough to try one. Brad lit it for him and Derrick cautiously inhaled. When his eyes watered and his cheeks tightened, he coughed. Brad laughed, "You'll get the hang of it, I'm sure of it." He sounded like a jerk, like all those guys at school who didn't want anything to do with us. When Brad asked us what we'd been up to, we shrugged. Said something about school, where he hadn't shown his face for weeks. We weren't about to tell him anything.

$P$eople wrote letters to the newspaper scrutinizing the whole idea of a public birth. They said that the swimmers had forgotten about the safety of the child. We tried not to dwell on what we knew. It was Tim who finally said it. We were walking to his house after school while the winds hinted at an evening storm. "Was it Brad's—you know?"

We shrugged our shoulders. Derrick said it for all of us. "No." It was supposed to make us feel better, so why didn't it work? For the first time, we wanted to forget the swimmers that made our town special; we wanted to forget what we had seen.

We were sure they'd stop performing. Townspeople no longer attended the show out of memory of that fateful Saturday. Most said the swimmers ought to mourn, and that it was too soon to return to the water. We took to loitering outside the ticket booth. One of these Saturdays it was just the three of us and we were making plans to steal a can of beer or two from one of our fathers' stashes and go to the park, past the warm can, when we happened to glance at the shore and saw Mariona step up. She unzipped her shorts, pulled off her shirt and strolled across the beach in her black suit, the ends of her hair just grazing her shoulders. We were immediately transfixed; we stood shoulder to shoulder and clutched the fence with our hands. Her parents beamed, applauded her initial strokes, then turned to watch Mariona pull herself effortlessly onto the shark's back. She lifted her arms up until they arched over her head, placed her hands on the great white and kicked her legs up into a handstand. Together they skimmed the water for several minutes. The crowd gave her a standing ovation. We jumped up and down, high-fived one another. Mariona was back!

Two days later, we saw Brad sitting on the lawn in front of school, his legs kicked out before him. We told him Mariona was again performing, and then said, "We're going to the boardwalk." He took a drag off a cigarette, flung it from his fingers. It hit the sidewalk and rolled, a sliver of smoke still rising.

"I'm busy." He lifted himself off the grass. "Send Mariona my good wishes." Brad slapped Tim on the side of the head.

"Ouch! Jerk!"

Brad mimicked Tim and walked away. We decided not to go to the boardwalk that night. What if we saw Mariona? We couldn't talk to her after what Brad had done.

Years later we still don't understand her final show. Mariona seemed pleased to return to the water. "Maybe she did it for him. Her boyfriend didn't look like the swimming type," mentioned Derrick. He recalled her passion for fortunes.

"How well could she really do it?" asked Tim, whose parents eventually divorced. The rest of us thought she might have actually seen into the future. What else could explain that spectacular Saturday, with its brilliant sun and billowing clouds, the day she retired from swimming for good?

School was out for the summer and soon all of us would be seniors, deciding between the army and navy or going to work at the glass plant with our fathers. One of us would end up taking a class at the community college, even fewer would get out of town, like Mariona, although we still hoped her predictions for our lives would become true.

We sneaked into the audience of her final show. Mariona started the performance, a rarity. She took to the water in a burst of energy, blitzing through the waves alongside the sharks, kicking with grace and power. We'd bought glossy photos of her from the souvenir booth for ten dollars apiece, and each of us joked we'd wait until after the show and get her autograph no matter what. We held our pictures in hand, careful to touch only the edges. In the water, Mariona placed one hand on the shark's side and wrapped her right hand around its fin. She waved at the audience, her teeth gleaming stars. Mariona held onto the shark's tail fin for some time before hauling herself onto its back, anticipating the waves and motions of the shark with skill and mastery. She soared over the water. We hooted, applauded until our palms stung, yelled at the top of our lungs. The water beaded off her like rain and she glimmered as sleek as the animal she had almost tamed.

She held a handstand for four minutes. We timed her. But then this is where our accounts differ. Someone from the paper reported it was a giant wave from one of the ferries offshore. Derrick said she misplaced her foot when she tried to stand on the shark. But a few of us, a careful few, think she purposefully flung herself off the shark and into the choppy, blue-green waves. We saw a leg cut up into the shark's gills and it tilted its massive mouth to the side. It refrained from movement until Mariona's fist slammed the shark right beneath its left eye. We heard the smack on its thick skin. Then, the shark rolled its black eyes backwards and opened its jaws, serrated teeth long accustomed to the taste of tuna and dolphin. It only took one bite, one chunk of flesh before releasing its jaws and leaving Mariona in the water, inhaling frantically on her back.

Later that summer, we found out Brad impregnated a girl one town over. One night the girl's father came to his house while it was raining, demanding Brad marry her. The man pushed his fist into Brad's nose and by the time the rain stopped the following day, Brad was gone.

Mariona lost her left foot up to the ankle. For years afterward she continued to show up on the shore during Saturday afternoons, her boyfriend alongside her. She took to wearing a white high top on her left foot, some kind of orthopedic appliance tucked inside. She strode in the same strong way and her hips compensated for the lost inch with a slight tilt. Together, Mariona sat in the bleachers with her boyfriend and watched the show with the rest of us and everyone forgot that they were even there, that Mariona once was the entire performance.

Mariona set up her own fortune telling booth on the boardwalk, although we never visited her there. We gave up on the reading of our futures. At some point Mariona and her boyfriend moved away and we lost track of them. We can imagine that Mariona has her own little girl now and that she takes her swimming in the ocean and together they float on their backs looking up at the sky.

The shark swimmers never were the same after Mariona's last swim. Their suits grew shabbier, dingy. Her father began spending his time at Kilroy's bar and his wife began to shrivel away. At some point it was no longer worth watching their tired bodies toss in the surf. They retired and put the act to rest.

That day, though, has remained in our minds. Mariona's final show. We were there. We watched the ambulances scream on the sand, saw her mother hysterically wailing as her husband carried Mariona out of the water and onto the land, his daughter's blood cloaking his arm and torso, streaks dribbling from his swimsuit down his own legs. Mariona's face was ghostly white—she'd already fainted. We stood there in our own circle in the bleachers, watching. The wind bent our photos of Mariona into halves, flicking them in quick succession, nearly ripping them from our knotted fists.

# Bejeweled

*D*evola would be the first to admit she didn't understand how her life so drastically changed course. What she knew for certain was that the trembling of misfortune began when the manager of Good Foods caught her with her hands inside the stock boy's pants, leaning against the cantaloupes, nowhere near the register she was paid to attend. She lost her job and ended up at a bar off Interstate 80. Eight days and many bottles of Coors later, she arrived in Brewster, Iowa, with a husband twenty-seven years her senior, the stench of cow manure seeping into her skin. That was eleven months ago.

During what Devola planned would be her final day in Iowa, she stood with her lover in the bedroom of her husband's house. Anders fanned the air in front of his nose. "Your things are zoo-scented," he said. "We're going to have to buy you all new clothes in Chicago."

She sniffed her shirt. "I can't even smell it anymore."

Anders shook his head. "I haven't yet lost hope in you." He rolled onto the side of the bed closest to Devola and motioned at her. "It's going to be such a long day," he said and pulled her back onto the mattress.

"Seventeen hours," she added. "And then we're outta here." Just thinking about it made her shiver.

Downstairs, something heavy dragged across the floor.

Devola shot up. "Did you hear something?" She poked her head outside the bedroom. "Gus? That you?"

"Shit. I thought you said Gus was at auction all day." Anders sprung off the bed and grabbed his pants.

"He's supposed to be." She tucked in her blouse and finger combed her hair. "Don't forget your mail bag this time."

Devola skittered down the stairs. "Honey, you finish early?" She peered out the windows where the corn stalks shook in the breeze and the air conditioner hummed. She didn't see any one. "Sweetie?" In the living room, the maple-trimmed armchair stood away from its place near the window. Devola laid a hand on one of the chair's arms and the olive velour seat split open like a pair of lips, pushing out a pearl necklace. Just as quickly, the opening sealed shut. Devola dropped onto her knees and inspected the jewelry lying on the cushion with as calm a countenance as a piece of lint. She fingered the shimmery beads and hefted their weight in her hands. She hunched over and called upstairs. "Anders, it's all clear."

Dressed as a postal carrier, Anders's muscular legs appeared twice their size in the pleated shorts, the fake mailbag they'd stuffed with newspapers hanging off his shoulder. "Look at this." She held up the necklace. "It came out of this chair."

Anders squinted. "That upholstery is too atrocious for anyone to hide anything inside. Shoot, I would have tossed that homely thing years ago."

"It was a wedding gift from Gus's mom," said Devola.

He bit the necklace. "They seem real enough, but they can't be. Surely she would be the last person to bribe *you* to marry Gus."

Devola didn't quite follow, but before she could think about his comment, Anders squeezed her waist. "We'll leave for the windy city tomorrow morning at eight. Then all your fairy tale wishes shall come true." He waved an imaginary wand over her head. At the back door, she straightened his shirt collar.

"I hope your route's good!" she joked. He mock-saluted her and left. She watched his head disappear out the back door and then, since it was her last full day in Brewster, Devola popped open a can of Budweiser; it burned her throat all the way down. She sipped from the can, and returned to the chair. Placing the beer on the floor, she leaned over and rubbed both chair arms. The cushion's lips tore even wider and this time spit out a diamond tennis bracelet and a sapphire ring that fit her fourth finger perfectly. She held it out, admiring the sapphire's luster. When she and Anders married, he could give her this ring.

Suddenly she heard the rumbling of Gus's truck. Devola pushed the chair against the wall, pocketed the bracelet and ring, and rushed upstairs to shower.

For dinner, she and Gus had tacos and between bites her husband asked if she cut her hair. "No," she said. "Why?"

"You look different," he said. "A nice different."

"Thanks." She concentrated on adding more salsa to her taco and hid her grin; it was the heavy diamond bracelet in her pocket that made her radiant.

That night, while Gus buzzed and snored, she slipped into her pink chenille robe. As soon as her feet touched the carpet in the living room, the groaning began. "Sshh! You'll wake him," she whispered. The chair scooted itself into the middle of the room, the seat cushion illuminated by a fat block of moonlight. Devola fell on her knees and lightly rubbed its arms. A warm tingling passed over her. She undid her robe and squashed her bare chest against the seat cover. Devola had never had a child, but she could imagine what it would be like to breast-feed, the incessant tugging and release. The chair shuddered, opened its lips and for a moment, Devola roamed around inside its padding. She panted. A pair of diamond earrings tumbled onto the floor. She held them up to the glow of the moon. "They are the loveliest of all," she said, and reached around and hugged the chair. Devola took a blanket from the hall closet and made herself a bed on the floor, her head underneath the chair's rungs. Together, they slept in the circle of their own quiet.

In the morning, Devola's hand reached for the cramp at the back of her neck. She massaged the skin, then placed her hand on the carpeting where an array of stones pricked her palm—an emerald brooch, a pearl ring, three gold herringbone chains and even a diamond tiara with a ruby trim. Devola scooped them up and held them against her. "You'll spoil me." She moved out from beneath the chair and kicked off the blanket. "I'm not going anywhere, I promise you that." She smoothed the chair's seat and pattered into the kitchen to pour a cup of coffee. Gus's cereal bowl was on the table with milk still pooled at its bottom. Like a map, toast crumbs dotted the place where he'd eaten. She licked her finger and dabbed at the crumbs, then noticed it was already 7:30 a.m. What about Anders? Her self-proclaimed Prince Charming? Within the hour he would be in his Jeep, outside the Hamburg Inn, waiting for her.

As if it could read her mind, the chair groaned and Devola returned to its side. She found a Cartier watch resting beside it. "Now you've outdone yourself," she said. "What can I say?" She thought for a moment, resting her head on the chair's arms, and then lifted the chair so it faced her. Together, they headed up the stairs. Devola carried the chair into the guest room, its back to the window. Taking a brush from the dresser drawer, she started in on her hair, cutting through the knots until her hair cascaded down her back in one luminous wave. She kept her eyes on the seat cushion and removed her robe, dropping it at her feet. Goosebumps appeared. Her skin glimmered in the bright morning light. A sound escaped from the chair. It was low and soft, like a kitten freed from a closet.

It was as if the ground was moving and shaking beneath her feet. The town of Brewster and the entire world for that matter was being made over, and in a moment, when the rattling in Devola's chest stopped, she was certain everything would be different—reformed, new. The chair had been here all along. Everything became fiery as if Devola dangled from a rotisserie. "Tell me," she said, leaning toward the chair, her breath moist and warm. "What else do you have?"

# The Sisters
# in the Glass House

*H*e heard the waves bashing the lake's shore but he didn't stop walking until he was in front of the glass house where the town had imprisoned the sisters. The blinds were drawn on all sides. Salvador tiptoed up the gravel walkway lined with pots of red and white flowers. There was a painted mailbox with the sisters' first names, although it had been vandalized. In heavy blue spray it said: FREE THEM. Salvador found a place where the blinds left the window bare. He peered inside the glass house and noticed the two beds. One of them exposed a foot, the other held a lump of blankets. A chest of drawers separated the beds and a crumpled heap of clothes (blouses?) remained balled on the floor.

The glass house had been one of Salvador's first major contracts. The town initially planned to use it to display the latest appliances and furnishings available at local retailers. Every month the house would showcase a different merchant. During this time two girls were discovered hitchhiking along the highway. They were sisters, ages sixteen and eighteen. When the police questioned them, they spoke sarcastically, saying they were runaway orphans. Crime had slowly been escalating and the townspeople found it disturb-ing that these sisters sneered so easily at the police; if they hadn't yet done something illegal they certainly would at some point. The glass house seemed the perfect place for them.

Salvador's daughters, ages eight and nine, were no longer in-terested in coming down to the lakefront and watching the sisters. But his son, at the nimble age of five, was fascinated by the fact that the girls couldn't get out, that they lived their lives on display, and that the town had placed them there. On occasion there were picketers and student-groups that rallied for the girls' freedom, but to no avail. Too many old-timers lived in town, people who recalled how dangerous the town had been before they locked the sisters in the glass house.

*A*s a high school student, Salvador had black hair and black furious eyes. He kept his head down and squinted as if attempting to burn a hole in the ground. He wore black shirts and dark jeans and didn't like to shower. He and his father fought about chores, his grades, and the fact he hadn't made the football team. Once his father had shoved him so hard against his bedroom wall that a patch of paint the size of a fist chipped off. At fifteen, Salvador accepted a job at Fat Dan's Deli where he planned to save every penny he earned and move away, just as his mother had wisely done.

Memories of his mother were blurry, indistinct. Salvador had been a few months old when she left, so what he recalled were likely figments of his imagination. Sometimes he recalled his mother telling his father he was heartless, but he didn't know if this had actually occurred or if he simply hoped it had.

With such limited experience with girls, it surprised Salvador that he immediately felt drawn to Vanessa, the girl who worked the register at Fat Dan's. His father had told him countless times that women were liars and weren't to be trusted, yet from their earliest introduction, Vanessa seemed different. She wore a gold chain bracelet and as she rang up orders for corned beef sandwiches, she pressed the numbers on the register and it made a click-clack, like a light switched on and off. Salvador liked to think that his mother also had this same kind, strong-mindedness.

John Barleycorn was the cook at Fat Dan's. He had a tiger tattooed at the back of his neck and the second night on the job he told Salvador that Vanessa had a baby at home. "Her boyfriend's an ass. Real jerk. One time he came in here and started yelling at Dan. Wanted some free food and Dan said he had to pay for it like anyone else." John paused. He squatted on the concrete porch at the back of the deli. John smoked a cigarette, sucked on it so hard his lips made a popping sound.

Salvador looked at the sky. It was starting to snow softly, the flakes tickling his face like feathers.

"You got a girlfriend?" asked John Barleycorn.

Salvador stared at him.

John cupped a hand on his shoulder. "Nothing to be afraid of. I didn't lose my virginity until I was sixteen. That gives you how many years?"

"Hey. What's with you?" asked Salvador.

"Okay, bud. You don't have to tell me. But I'd say it'll be another year or two for you. Plenty of guys are much older when they lose it. They always survive and she isn't any wiser. Women don't know the difference. Unless you look like Dan." He lowered his voice. "Big bellies like his make it difficult sometimes."

Salvador's throat burned. "I can imagine."

Back inside, the radio said they were in for a good six inches of snow. For the third time that night, Dan showed Salvador how to wipe the floors. He took the mop from Salvador's hands. "Gimme. You've got to use more of your back. The mop won't bite you." He paused. "Your pop and I could bench two hundred pounds apiece when we were your age. Your dad says you're a sissy boy. It ain't true, is it?"

Dan kept mopping and said he'd finish the floor. There wasn't a single customer in line for fried chicken or tuna salad, so Dan told Vanessa to teach Salvador how to inventory the freezer. "And he learns slow so take your time." They both put on jackets and stepped in the giant icebox near the back entrance. The door heaved shut.

Salvador held a clipboard with all of the items the deli stocked and began reading. "Mozzarella?"

"Six chunks," said Vanessa.

"Butter?"

"One box of eight," said Vanessa. "You like working here?"

Unlike pictures he'd seen of his mother, Vanessa's hair was so blonde it was nearly white—everything about her was ghostly and pale—the button-down shirt she wore rolled at the elbows, the skin on her face. It was nearly translucent and crossed with veins. She yawned, pressed her thumbs into her eyelids as if her vision could be improved with force.

"It's all right," said Salvador.

"You go to Femley High, right?" she asked.

"Yeah," he responded.

"I went there for a few years. I wasn't much impressed. I'm gonna go to business college and learn how to be a receptionist. That's why this is a good place for me to work. I get to polish up on my people skills."

She stared at him and he realized she was waiting for a response. "That's nice," he said.

"What do you want to do when you're older?" he asked.

Salvador shrugged.

"Someday you will. You'll just reach this point and you'll know. Like me. I know myself. I can multi-task. That means I can handle more than one job at a time. All receptionists must be able to multi-task. I would have never known I could do this job until Dan gave me a chance. He's been better to me than any of my relatives."

He glared at the clipboard. He really didn't feel like talking.

The weeks blended together. Salvador cleaned the floors and wiped down the tables, restocked shelves and the freezer. And when Vanessa's back was turned he watched the way she carried herself, like a child who had been punished.

One evening, at the end of his shift, he punched out and waited at the back door. His father had said he'd pick him up. After half an hour he kicked the door and it swung wide. He started walking. Most likely his dad was trying to teach him a lesson. "Gotta be a man, Salvador," his father had said more times than he could count. "Can't be going around like you're clueless about what's between your legs."

Screw him, thought Salvador. He would walk. Maybe he'd keep going and leave Homewood altogether. What would his father do if he had no one to push around?

"Hey, wait up!" Vanessa ran behind him, her feet slipping on the new, wet snow. She held her purse on her shoulder with one hand. "Where are you going? Can I come?" she asked.

He shrugged. "Suit yourself." He thrust his hands in his jacket pockets so hard it looked like he hid boulders. They walked along the backside of the plaza past Arthur's Hardware and Old Time Buffet. "Where's your ride?" he asked her.

"I'm not ready to go home. It's a nice night. I thought I'd

give you some company."

He felt his face redden. Whether she meant it or not he couldn't tell.

"Don't you have a ride?" she asked.

"My dad, the original jerk," he said. "He tries to make me lift weights at night. He'll stand there and count." It came out in a rush—he couldn't stop himself. "He's the one who got me this idiotic job. He and Dan played football when they were in high school and that's exactly what he wants me to do." When he finished he gulped, his mouth dry.

She crossed her arms. "What? Sucks to be you. Is that what you want to hear? You think you're the only one with problems?" She sniffled and rubbed her nose. "Shoot, kid. I left my folks when I was years younger than you. Don't you know how you start out doesn't matter?" A car horn bleated behind them. Vanessa jumped. "That's me," she said. "I've got to go." She grasped the edge of her purse and jogged toward the long car, her jacket flinging open and slipping off one shoulder as if that was exactly what it was supposed to do.

Salvador crossed his legs and leaned his head against the backside of a park bench. He watched the rising and falling of his chest and tried to relax. With his eyes closed it became easier to hear the lapping waves, ticking lamplights, and a soft wheezing— one of the sisters? He squinted, tried to guess which girl would be a noisy sleeper. He had forgotten their names. There was an engraved wood sign with white letters a few feet from him that described the history of the sisters. He didn't have the energy to get up and read it. He knew the older one was a few inches taller and supposedly the stricter of the two, while a few years ago the younger girl had tried to escape. In his experience, most girls weren't so persistent.

Salvador's daughters came when called. Their hair gleamed, smelled of vanilla. He knew they liked to read fairy tales and play house in their shared bedroom. All of his children smiled, said please, and only fought with one another during Saturday morning cartoons.

While the town had intended for the sisters to serve as an example to potential criminals, clearly the sisters also warned others of the dangers of an immoral life. For years word had spread that Homewood had locked up two hitchhikers and would do the same to other offenders who tried to live so brazenly. The first time Salvador had taken his son to the park he had carried him on his shoulders. His daughters had run ahead and were tapping on the glass, making faces at the sisters. As Salvador approached the glass with his son, the boy began to sob, warm tears dropping onto Salvador's thinning black hair. "What? What happened?" he asked. Salvador sat down on the same bench where he currently rested. He took his son into his arms and held him until he quieted.

Finally his son spoke. "Will they lock me up too?"

Salvador held himself back from laughing. "No. Not you. You're perfect. These girls didn't have anywhere else to go. They like being here. See?" The sisters were playing cards and the younger one, with her hair piled on top of her head, laughed wildly. His son looked doubtful. In the glass house they had a spacious apartment, a monthly stipend, food, and paid utilities. And they kept Homewood safe; they needn't worry about any wackos. He tried to explain this to his son, but as he spoke he became less certain of what he was saying. When he peered closer at the sisters' faces, Salvador noticed the tiny lines, their plastic smiles.

For the first time he wondered if they were happy.

He glanced away, became fixed on the sight of his son's drying tears, the streaks on his face like a dried-up riverbed, reminding him of the last time he himself had cried, how the release had felt like something inside him had broken.

*T*hroughout the winter of his sophomore year Salvador had worked at Fat Dan's Deli. Twice he'd threatened to quit and his father said if he did, he should pack a bag and call his grandmother in South Dakota. The only part of the deli he enjoyed was Vanessa. The hours at work dragged if she called in sick or if she had to shuttle between counters, hustling to meet customer demands. When it was busy, a thin bead of sweat dotted her upper lip, which made Salvador's stomach curl. She should be home, he thought, studying for her receptionist degree. Secretly, though John Barleycorn had said Vanessa had a baby, Salvador liked to think it was a rumor, that in reality, no matter how difficult life had been for Vanessa, she hadn't let it beat her. So he ignored Dan's criticisms of the way he mopped the floors or scrubbed the toilet. Instead, he pretended he was making money for the apartment he and Vanessa would share in California or some other faraway place.

One particularly slow night John Barleycorn taught him to smoke cigarettes and when Salvador succeeded without coughing, John swatted his back and said, "Nice work. Iron lungs, that's what you've got. People kill for those." Salvador flushed with the compliment.

When he came inside Vanessa motioned for him to join her behind the deli counter. She scooped orange Jell-O into a bowl and handed it to him. "Guess what?" she asked.

"I don't have a clue."

"C'mon. Try," said Vanessa.

Salvador sighed. "You inherited money from a long-lost relative."

"I already told you I'm not in contact with anyone I'm related to."

"I forgot," said Salvador. "I give up."

"Too easily, that's for sure." She poked his side with an elbow, then pulled out a piece of ivory paper and handed it to him. The heading at the top read: "Sawyer College of Business" and in the center of the page was a date and time. He handed it back to her. "I've got an interview for admission to the college next week. And I'm really good at interviews. Plus I have this beige suit I found for half-price at JCPenny. They aren't going to be able to say no."

Salvador congratulated her.

"They also teach you computer skills and stuff. Who knows where this will take me? But don't worry. If I own a company and you need a job, I promise to hire you."

"Really?" his legs tingled.

"Sure. You still have to work and everything, but I'll give you an office."

"Thanks. I guess you should know my grades aren't anything great."

Vanessa rolled her eyes and pretended to spit on the floor. "That's what I think about school. It's no indicator of nothing. I think you'll be a great addition to my company."

"Unless I raise my grade point average, my dad's kicking me out when I turn seventeen," he said.

"You'll be fine," said Vanessa. "Not a doubt in my mind. People like us take care of ourselves." She play-punched him. "You can always stay on my couch."

Salvador worked to steady himself; the weight of his heart threatened to push him over.

"What would your boyfriend say?" interrupted John

Barleycorn, hovering behind them, his arm propped on the meat slicer.

"Shut up, John. You don't know a thing about me," said Vanessa.

"Lies. Lies. I seen him lurking around. Are you embarrassed or something? Salvador's a man of the world. He understands these things."

Salvador looked at her. Was it true?

"Idiot," she spat.

That meant that it was true. Or that John Barleycorn was exaggerating.

Dan appeared. "How's our family doing?"

"Grand. This is the best Christmas ever, Dad," said John Barleycorn.

"Well, I know you've all been good." Dan hit three buttons on the register. It chirped and the drawer popped open. He filled the maroon bank bag, and then went into his office. "Salvador, I told you to refill the soap dispensers, didn't I?"

Salvador stomped away. If Vanessa had a boyfriend she'd tell him, wouldn't she? Grabbing a bucket and mop from the floor of the storage closet he pulled a can of scouring powder off a shelf. He looked over at Vanessa. She was spraying the glass deli case, her mouth a frazzled line like the strands of the mop before he dunked it in to the pail of soapy water. He scoured the sink, tip-toed to the front of the deli. He kept his voice low. "Is he always such a jerk?"

"Which one?" she asked.

"Dan the man," said Salvador.

"Oh, I don't know. He's just particular."

The bells at the front of the deli chimed and Salvador, figuring it was a customer, headed toward the bathroom.

"What are you doing here?" he heard Vanessa ask a moment later.

Salvador poked his head out of the bathroom and saw a man with a slender ponytail. The man said, "It's time to go, Vanessa. Now." He wore flip-flops even though the temperature was below zero.

Vanessa rubbed her hands on the front of her apron and Dan and John Barleycorn appeared. From where he stood near the bathroom, Salvador could see her bite her lip.

Dan checked his watch and sighed. "She's on the clock until ten." He glanced at Vanessa who pressed her back between the deli counter and a stack of boxes. "Heck, this is her job. She's got another hour. And if you don't like that . . . ." Dan threw up his hands.

"You can't tell her what to do." The man tugged on his ponytail.

"Like hell I can't." Dan turned to Vanessa. "I can't just let you come and go when you please. I need someone who's reliable. I'm not running a charity." She didn't say anything, fumbled with her apron tie and took her purse out of the office. She placed the thin strap on her shoulder and walked toward the man whose nose looked like a hook that'd been hung incorrectly; he jerked her arm and she winced. Dan stepped up under the man's chin. "Leave her alone or I'll call the police."

"Go ahead, Fatso," he spat.

"Please, Dan. Just this once." Vanessa placed herself between Dan and the man, touching his shoulder with the tips of her purple nails.

The man dragged her toward the door, and Vanessa kept looking back. He finally said to her, "It's now or never, babe. You pick."

"Bye everyone," she waved, her voice light and peppery, the

bells chiming again.

"What do you think of that?" asked John.

"I don't know why she's with him. She could do so much better," said Dan.

"Who was that?" asked Salvador, stepping forward.

"Salvador, do you remember how babies are made?" asked John Barleycorn. "He's the baby's daddy."

Dan screwed up his eyebrows. "How do you know that?"

"Everyone knows that," said John Barleycorn.

Salvador mopped the bathroom floor. Maybe she was so lonely she didn't realize good guys existed. She didn't need to stay with the man just because he was the baby's daddy—if indeed he was the baby's daddy. Although Salvador didn't know anything about love, there had been a girl in the fifth grade he liked to sit beside during reading hour. She had moved away. And what had Salvador ultimately learned? That the people he cared for always disappeared.

Salvador stared at his reflection in the bathroom mirror, his eyes like pieces of coal. John Barleycorn poked his head inside. "Another lesson for you, Sal. Choose wisely. Some of these broads are bonkers." He twirled a finger along the side of his head. "And that one's certifiable."

"Fuck you, John."

"Ooh! Sorry! I forgot about your relationship. Maybe you finally stuck something down the rabbit hole?"

"Lay off the kid," yelled Dan. "Let him do his work."

They both deserved a fist shoved down their respective throats. "You couldn't hurt a fly," is what his father said the last time Salvador's report card arrived and he'd held him against the wall.

His father was right. He couldn't hurt a fly. But he could save someone and that was far more important.

No matter how well he explained it, Salvador's wife would never understand what had happened at the deli. Salvador barely comprehended it himself. Yet his wife had a way of not hearing him, like the time one of his daughters had gotten into a fight. His wife had stepped out into the backyard to find his daughter pummeling the chest of the Barker girl. After tearing the two girls apart, his wife had made them apologize and play a game of Monopoly. Later that evening when Salvador heard what happened, he was furious on two counts—first, that his daughter had been fighting and second, that his wife let the two girls spend the rest of the afternoon together. That night he forbade both his daughters from playing with the Barker girl or any other neighbor.

His wife had snickered as he made the announcement. "Do you want them to be hermits like you?" she asked. "You can't protect them from everything."

Two days later he saw both his daughters riding bikes with the Barker girl. They waved as they passed him. He'd rushed into the house and questioned his wife. "Didn't I tell you I wanted the girls to stay away from the neighbors?"

She stared at him, and said quietly, "I guess I didn't hear you."

And it was the truth. They didn't hear each other. While he knew he loved his wife, he didn't know if he liked her. He had weighted the merits of marriage through other means.

Life with Vanessa would have been different. If Salvador and Vanessa had married they would have moved away and explored the world. Their lives would have been colorful and worth remembering and maybe there would be less rules. Instead he designed buildings and although he'd done better than his father ever predicted, it wasn't enough. He couldn't sleep anymore. Vanessa's image traipsed through his mind forcing him to guzzle mugs of coffee between clients, his head bobbing into his chest while he waited in traffic. Perhaps someday he'd fall asleep at the wheel. What did Vanessa want from him? What do you want from me? He screamed at the stars.

$T$he day following Vanessa's interview she had stood behind the counter filling napkin dispensers. When Salvador arrived she looked up and he could not turn away from her face. It was as if someone had taken a brush and painted heavy rings on her face, bulging bruises made the blue of her eyes more vibrant. The corners of her mouth turned up for a moment, and then settled back into a flat line. Words writhed on his tongue. He asked what had happened.

"It was nothing. I slipped on some ice." He reached a hand toward her, and then halted it mid-air, turned away.

He excused himself, stepped outside in the back alley. John Barleycorn leaned against the brick wall, smoking. They stood there together not saying anything. Something about the cigarette smoke cleared his head, helped Salvador focus. He returned inside determined to speak with Vanessa.

"How'd your interview go?" he asked her.

Vanessa fingered the buttons of the register. "Tuition is more than I thought. It's a lot of money."

"You could get a loan. That's what my dad does. He lends people money for things they can't afford."

"No one would give me money."

"I would."

She shook her head no. "Someday I'll go. Now's just not the right time."

He already planned to share his earnings with her. They would move away together, maybe even get a dog. Salvador would be a good father to Vanessa's baby. He could see all of it so clearly, yet she was dating some asshole that used her face as a punching bag. Blood rose in his head, buzzed in his ears. "Do you want to work at Fat Dan's the rest of your life? You have a baby to consider and you're going to shrug all that aside because the time isn't right?"

She sucked in a mouthful of air. "I'm not who you think I am. You don't know me. You don't know what goes on inside my head."

"I don't need to know. I've seen you with people," said Salvador, "You're good. That's all that matters."

"You two trying to solve the world's problems again?" asked John Barleycorn.

Vanessa glared at him.

"Sure was nice to see your boyfriend in here the other day. The years agree with him. The years outside the penitentiary, that is."

Vanessa stomped past John Barleycorn, slammed the bathroom door.

"I don't know what you see in her, kid," said John Barleycorn.

"Well, I don't see what you don't." Salvador straightened one of the tables.

"Touché." John Barleycorn picked something out from between his teeth and flung it into the garbage. "Dan told me to tell you to clean the front windows, and then inventory the pantry with your sweetheart."

Salvador went into the backroom and pulled on his parka. He filled a bucket with ammonia and hot water. Outside, he swished a squeegee in the mixture and started on the windows. While he worked, he watched Vanessa and John Barleycorn exchange words. Although he couldn't discern what she said, her mouth moved fast. A flood of heat stirred beneath his jacket. She was probably telling him off. About time, he thought.

Salvador blew on his hands; the skin had transformed into a chalky red. He wondered how quickly a person could get frostbitten. If his fingers fell off there'd likely be months of rehabilitation. He wouldn't be able to continue working at Fat Dan's and the thought pleased him. He imagined Vanessa visiting him in the hospital with a bouquet of flowers, the two of them alone in his room.

In the pantry, Vanessa and Salvador worked in near silence, Salvador checking off items from the list and Vanessa counting. At last, she spoke. "I've been thinking about what you said."

He looked up at her.

"And I think you're right. About time and all. That if I really want something I've got to act now. It makes a lot of sense."

He nodded. "I don't mean to interfere."

"No, you're a good friend and that's what I needed to hear," said Vanessa.

"I know things aren't always so simple for you," said Salvador, "with the baby and all."

"And you should know that doesn't really matter."

Dan popped his head in. "Vanessa? Your boyfriend's here. I already escorted him outside. If he has something to say to you he can do it on the sidewalk. You have five minutes."

"But—"

"No buts this time. We've been over this. I'll tell him you'll be with him in a few."

Salvador grabbed her hands. "Vanessa—let him go. Please."

"What are you doing?" she asked.

"You don't have to stay with him," said Salvador. "I can help you and the baby. I have money. I can send you to Sawyer Business College."

"What are you doing? Steve's my boyfriend. I love him. Let me go." She pushed him away and he stumbled, righted himself on a box of paper plates. Her eyebrows were twisted up into her forehead, one hand rubbing the skin he'd touched. "I don't know what's gotten into you, Salvador. But you're wrong. I've got to go."

Dan entered the pantry, slapped his hands together. "Where were you two?"

"Vanessa was counting."

"Good," said Dan. "Go on, I pick up quick."

"Tortillas?" asked Salvador.

"We've got a full box." Dan turned toward him. "Salvador, let me give you some advice. Be picky when you start dating. You'll save yourself and your father from a real headache." His voice softened. "She ever say anything to you about where she grew up?"

Salvador shook his head. The bells hanging from the cord on the front door collapsed on the floor in a muted sigh. Vanessa returned to the storage room and told Dan she wasn't feeling well. "You can call someone to pick you up if you like, but this is the last straw," said Dan. "You need to finish your shift, Vanessa. Two more hours."

She whimpered. Her face was puffy and wet and she reminded Salvador of a two-year-old. "I can do this myself," said Salvador. "Why don't you do something else?" She walked away rubbing her eyes. He listened to her sniveling in the other room and told himself she had a cold.

*T*he moon illuminated bits of white foam. Salvador took off his loafers and walked along the shore, the cold sand needling between his toes. When he stopped he noticed the roof of the glass house, the see-through ceiling that he'd designed. The ends of his pants dampened and tapered. He changed directions, walked away from the streetlights where the beach curved out into a bow, water surrounding his field of vision. When he thought of Vanessa it all seemed such a tragedy. If she had let him help her he would have done all that he could. Even now, he was certain of it.

*A*fter school, Salvador went home. His father was still at work. Salvador knew that the idea he'd been kicking around was the right thing to do. He took his savings account booklet from his father's drawer. He had saved over two thousand dollars in his college account; the result of every paycheck and birthday gift he'd ever received. When the teller at the savings and loan asked how he wanted his funds, Salvador replied, "Cash. In twenties and fifties."

His father would erupt with rage when he received the letter in the mail showing the account's balance at zero. Salvador looked forward to his fury. He felt as if he could wrestle a lion. What did his father know about being a man? This, emptying his savings account, would liberate Vanessa from her boyfriend. Who had his father saved?

*T*hat night there was a basketball game in town and the players jammed Fat Dan's. At one point, Dan asked Salvador to help Vanessa with the orders. He pushed plastic utensils and napkins into paper bags while she spoke with the customers. A thin curtain of sweat decorated Vanessa's forehead and a line of customers wove past the water fountain and still, Vanessa greeted each of the boys with a smile. Most of them were a year or two older than Salvador, although he recognized some of them from school.

"What can I get for you?" she asked a senior point guard.

"How about some chicken salad and a side of you. I'll provide the mayo."

Vanessa's fingers hung above the register buttons. "Screw you," she said.

"Why don't you?" said the point guard.

Salvador spun around. "What did you say?" Without thinking, he leapt over the counter, as if he was catching a touchdown pass. His middle fixed on top of the glass counter and he shoved his fist into the guy's nose. Vanessa screamed and Dan ran out, grabbing Salvador at the waist and pulling him off the counter.

"I was only joking, sir," said the point guard, scratching the front of his hair with his fingers, a narrow line of red trickling from his nostril.

"Fucking prick!" yelled Salvador.

Dan held both his elbows behind him, and pushed Salvador into the back room. "What's the matter with you?" Farther off, Salvador heard the same boy call Vanessa a slut. "I'm going to can your butt," said Dan. "Hear that? Your dad's a good friend, but this is a business."

"I'll save you the time," said Salvador, "I quit."

"That's up to you," said Dan. He told him to finish the night and then he huffed into his office and turned up the volume on the radio.

Later, his right fist covered by a bag of ice, Salvador tossed the last few bags of garbage in the dumpster, listening to their heft smacking against one another. Vanessa snuck up behind him. "That was nice, what you did tonight," she said.

"Stupid jocks." He tried not to look at her, knew one glance would wipe him out. She had said she loved her boyfriend and the words still lingered near.

"It seems like they're multiplying," she said.

"Hey. I almost forgot something. Stay here."

"I've got to go soon," said Vanessa.

"Just wait a minute, okay?" Salvador jogged inside and grabbed his backpack from Dan's office. He fished inside it for the thick envelope. He held the money from his savings account between both palms and it felt like he was making some kind of promise to her.

When he pushed the back door open he saw Vanessa leaning into the rolled-down window of the long car, twisting the toe of her shoe back and forth on the pavement. He watched the driver's hand touch her cheek and her own expression blossom. She pulled open the passenger's side door and raised a feeble hand as the car turned away.

Salvador refused to wave back.

The following day he arrived to pick up his final check. Vanessa, John, and Dan were washing walls and listening to the radio. Dan was in a good mood and called him into his office, telling him he hoped he'd choose to stay on.

"I'm just here for my check and then I'm gone."

"If that's what you want." Dan threw up his hands. "Kids," he said. "I need your timecard."

Salvador sat at a folding table near the back of the store and tabulated his hours. Vanessa joined him beside the table. "You're awfully late," she said.

He sighed. "I'm only here for my last paycheck. I quit."

"You did? When? —"

"Yes. Doesn't matter," he said. "Why are you with him? Why do you let him shove you around?" He shot up onto his feet and waved a finger beneath her chin. She flinched. Salvador stepped back, sobered by the forward curl of her shoulders, the way she held her arms with the edges of her fingers.

"Who?" asked Vanessa.

"Your boyfriend—personal Satan—whoever he is."

"I've been on my own a long time. Loneliness is the worst. Steve's not perfect, but I know he wants what's best for me." She took his hand and squeezed it. "We're friends, Salvador, right?"

He nodded.

"Listen. Something's going to take place here very soon. It'll be quick, and then everything will be ten times better. But first I need you to go into the freezer and stay there. I'll let you out when it's all clear. Twenty minutes, tops."

"What are you talking about?"

"Just do this for me, Sal. Please help me do this and then I'm done. I'm going to go to Sawyer Business College—didn't I tell you? We figured out how I can get money for tuition."

"You're crazy. I'm outta here—"

"Shhh. Please. It'll only be a few minutes. I'm sorry, Salvador. Help me do this. We'll hang out later, okay?"

"What's going on?" he asked.

She held the freezer door open, pushed him inside.

"I almost forgot," said Salvador. "I've got something for you. I tried to give it to you last night."

"Please, Salvador," said Vanessa. "Please go." She looked up at the clock on the wall, placed her hands on his shoulders, and urged him inside. The door dragged shut. Cloistered by ice and frozen groceries, everything muffled. He hugged his knees to his chest, the last song on the radio slipping through his brain, the melody of the guitar playing over and over. He closed his eyes. Even if she were with the other guy, he would give her the money.

*T*hey burst into the deli, shouting. Salvador woke with a jerk;

his head crooked to the side, a burn ripping along his neck. He tried to speak but his words remained lodged. When he tried to swallow, his throat felt as dry as paper. He cleared the face of his watch with his thumb—nearly midnight. Salvador coughed again, "I'm in—" he said, but was interrupted by the heavy swing of the freezer door, the warmth of the deli rushing in along with the smell of cold cuts and sliced cheese and the distant hum of the soda cooler. There were new sounds. Rubber-soled gym shoes and walkie-talkies. Had Dan booked a private party? No one was supposed to be in the back rooms. A rush of navy uniforms flanked Salvador. "You all right?" asked a man with a moustache like a rat's tail. The sound of tape being pulled and stretched. The police officer helped him to his feet, asked his name. "Who put you in the freezer?"

"She asked me." And already it seemed a lifetime ago. Salvador asked them what had happened. He followed the officer's wide back, his jowls pulsating with bubble gum. He told him there'd been a robbery. They stepped out of the freezer, and that is when Salvador turned, as if the warmth of the air suddenly woke him.

"Vanessa?" called Salvador. The officer headed toward the front of the deli while Salvador remained rooted. He saw her and his lungs emptied of air. She was curled up, a smear of pink against the wall where her head was partially propped, a pool of blood around the middle of her body. Two men were snapping photos; a third wore protective gloves and pulled instruments from some kind of metal box. One of her arms stretched out as if reaching for something over her head.

He yelled, felt it bounce off the walls, ricochet through his bones. The officers grabbed at his shoulders, yet Salvador was stronger than he'd ever been. He strained toward her, crawling, while the uniformed men yelled, told him not to touch her.

"Damn it! Stay put!" they said.

Salvador twisted his torso back and forth until one arm broke free and he dove toward her. He grabbed Vanessa's small fingers, already changing blue-gray. Her bracelet was pushed up in the middle of her forearm. He nudged it down to her wrist, smoothing the chain back and forth. Too late. Too early. He had been both.

"Come on," said the officer with the moustache. He turned Salvador's shoulders away. "Don't look. These are things you don't want to see." There was another group of uniformed men in Dan's office pointing cameras at the floor and taking pictures. The officer directed him past the glass deli counter with the fresh parsley trimmings Vanessa had probably arranged hours ago. He pulled out a chair for Salvador and gave him a glass of water. He sipped it, held it between two hands. When his father came in, Salvador did not recognize him. He seemed to exist in another reality altogether. He leaned over the table where Salvador sat and put a hand on his back. His father was wearing a green sweatshirt with a grease stain across one sleeve and he asked if Salvador was okay.

You were right, thought Salvador. I am not much of a man. His eyes filled like pools of ink. And sorrow settled in his bones.

Salvador hiked back toward the bench, brushed the sand off his feet, and put on his shoes. He had not forgotten the lesson he had learned. He stood in front of the glass house and cupped his hands around his mouth. "Sisters! Hey sisters!" he called.

Two blinds separated, and then the entire panel flew up in a whoosh.

He stood there looking at the sisters. The younger one propped a hand on her hip while the older sister leaned over from her bed, wide-eyed. "Tell me," he said, "is this what you want?"

The sisters stared at him. Blinked. It was suddenly clear—the memory of Vanessa prodding, urging him to visit the sisters in the middle of the night. Couldn't he save one girl in his lifetime?

Twenty feet from the water fountain, he noticed a red box standing upright. It said: "In case of fire, break." He kicked the glass in with the point of his shoe and yanked out the metal rim of the hose. The alarm seared his ears as Salvador ran toward the glass house. He swung the hose in a circle; it gained momentum, and then sailed through the side of the house. The thick glass fell away in jagged chunks, slamming onto the pavement, knocking the sign that held the history of the sisters on its side.

The front wall cleared of glass and the blinds shivered in the wind. Salvador stood there, hose in hand. The fire sirens wailed, yet he stood. The sisters stared at him expectantly. The youngest one cleared her throat. "Hey, gimme a hand," she said.

Salvador used the soles of his shoes to clear a path through the glass fragments and then reached around the middle of the younger sister. She was dressed in sneakers and stretchy pants. The older one was less eager to join them. "Come on," he told her.

"It's now or never, sis," said the younger sister. Then to Salvador, she said, "She's afraid of heights."

Salvador held out his arms, promised the older sister he would catch her. When she jumped, he held tight to her. Her feet touched ground and she galloped behind the younger sister, along the lakefront, the curling surf disguising their footprints. The fire trucks and patrol cars careened beyond them. Doors opened and slammed. Vanessa had asked him to go into the freezer and he'd done it. Salvador peeled off his jacket and began running behind the sisters, pumping his arms. The wind sloughed his skin, the air already burning in his lungs. He wouldn't stop unless they did. He'd keep running until they arrived safely. It was the least he could do.

# The Attached Couple

After a night of lovemaking, skin thrives. It was the only explanation that Julia could offer for why her and Kip's bodies had expanded, an opaque bridge of skin connecting at their waists. In the honeymoon suite at the Hotel Watiki, the windows reached the ceiling and were covered with a sheer white fabric more decoration than utility; the brightness burned Julia's eyes. She stuck her head beneath the sheet and examined the flesh. Overnight, their bodies had met in the middle, a thick four-inch wide space of flesh. Julia touched it, where her skin and Kip's had grown together. It was smooth and warm and she could feel the faint beat of her pulse or his pulse, she wasn't sure—it didn't matter. Julia had waited six and one-half years to become Mrs. Kip Kipplinger and nothing was going to ruin the beginning of their married life.

She propped herself up with her right arm, farthest from Kip, his shoulder tilting toward her. She wiggled her tongue back and forth over his earlobe, tugged on the cartilage between her teeth. He sloppily patted the back of her head, his fingers toppling into her nose and forehead. Good morning, Mr. Kipplinger, whispered Julia. She would never love anyone—not even herself—as much as she loved Kip. Julia watched as Kip tried to roll onto his left side. The attached flesh and the weight of her body kept him moored on his back.

He spoke in a warbled jumble, Let me go.

Sweetie, said Julia. I'm not doing anything. Something's come up.

Kip cleared his throat, jerked away from her suddenly, and yelled, Ouch! What the hell? Part of Julia's body—her arm and leg and one butt cheek landed on Kip's right side. He palmed Julia off him and his own body fell flat onto the mattress. He opened his eyes. The sheet crumpled to their hips and she watched him gaze at her nakedness. Julia was so close it felt as if she could feel the processes of his body.

Dear God! yelled Kip. He fixed on the new flesh between them and pulled at his half of the skin.

Aggh! screamed Julia.

He grabbed the headboard and tugged fiercely, pulling his body away from hers. Julia scrambled closer to where Kip held on. He backed farther away. Stay where you are! His knuckles rippled white, his face reddening; the skin joining them paled, drained of blood.

That hurts, she said, kicking his backside with a heel.

Kip tried chopping the flesh between their waists with his hand.

We're going to bruise! said Julia. Quit it! He was breathing fast, the insistent surf toppling and bashing together, like the Honolulu beach that could be heard faintly over the hum of the air conditioner. Julia kneeled, placed a cool palm on the back of his neck. We're married. She said it solemnly, as if she were singing the first few bars of the national anthem.

We're attached, he said. This isn't my idea of till death do us part.

It's probably just the residue from last night's asti spumante, said Julia.

Kip groaned. He closed his eyes and dug his fingers into his eyelids. My head hurts.

Let's go back to sleep. When we wake up everything'll be fine.

Julia! Go back to sleep? We wake up—he gestured at their waists—like this and you want to snooze?

There's obviously a good reason why our bodies have stitched like this. If we're patient, it will all come to us in due time.

Patient?

Quit repeating everything I say, said Julia.

Well it's just so *good* I can't help myself. Now work with me here. He took Julia's hand and they eased out of the bed. They stood side by side for a moment becoming accustomed to the feeling of the floor beneath their feet. The sheet fell in a crumpled heap exposing the mass of nearly translucent flesh; it was a mixture of their pigments, Julia's olive coloring and Kip's paler porcelain blended to a creamy mushroom hue. The idea of their joined forms gave Julia the goosebumps.

Just stand firm, he said, leaning over and placing his hands on the ground. Instinctively, she squatted beside him. Kip sighed. You've got to stand or this won't work.

She had been head cheerleader in high school and knew how to firmly position her feet. Okay, she said.

Kip tilted over and his hands dangled above the floor.

Julia placed her hands on her hips and bent her knees. She gritted her teeth. Please hurry. It's throbbing.

Kip's fingers met the ground and he kicked into a handstand.

Julia fell forward. They both crumbled into a mess of arms and legs. Her eyes watered. Shoot! She rubbed the skin back and forth while its color returned. That stung. Really.

This time, said Kip, if you can hold onto something and stay grounded, I can turn the handstand into a flip and break this puppy off for good.

Julia listened to the air threading from Kip's lips; it thinned and bloomed into a maniacal drizzle. Conversely, she felt utterly alive. Julia had secretly always wanted to crawl up inside Kip, live inside his skin. Being attached to him was the next best thing. Just give it a day, she said. If nothing happens, if there's no clear reason for our growth, we can go to the hospital, see a plastic surgeon. But we can't take this into our own hands. This is not for us to decide.

Be realistic, Julia, he said. I don't know what this is, but it's no more a sign than anything else. Just let me try one more time. I'm sure I can separate us and we can save the insurance co-payment.

Julia traced Kip's cheek with the backside of her hand. He shuddered, eyes blue marbles, the whites faintly yellowed and overused.

No. Julia paused, and then spoke again. Honey? I need to use the bathroom.

Huh?

Bathroom, she replied.

Oh, he said. Standing was easy, walking less so. He directed, Left foot, right foot. Kip put an arm around her back as if they were in a three-legged race. They both stared at the toilet.

She lifted up the seat. Close your eyes.

Jules, we're married. I'm going to see you sometime.

Just close them.

Kip crouched down, straddled the bathtub and Julia squatted

over the toilet. When she finished, she brought them over to the sink and washed her hands, then grabbed a brush and started in on her hair. Where do I get all these knots? she asked. It's like during the night birds choose my head to nest.

Come on, let's get dressed. I'm famished. Kip pulled Julia out of the bathroom. They walked by a complimentary bowl of fruit and he grabbed a mango. Want some?

Julia shook her head and watched him break the reddish shell with his bare hands. Juice dribbled down his forearms. I'm famished, he said, mouth full of yellow mush.

You already said that. They both pulled on shorts but were not sure what to do about the upper halves of their bodies. Julia bent over to fasten her bra and snatched a fitted green polo. Kip grabbed a T-shirt and pulled out a pocketknife. We'll just have to cut the sides a bit.

Julia yanked her shirt to her chest. I spent three hundred dollars on new clothes for this trip and you aren't going to ruin all of them.

What's your bright idea? Kip's voice was edgy and fast. He started waving his arms over his head, gesturing wildly. Tell me. What are we going to do?

Julia found herself following the aimless direction of his fingers. They looked helpless joined to his mad hands. This was not how she imagined their honeymoon. Julia didn't wait six years to marry a man whose voice pounded like heavy artillery against hers. Tears welled up, making narrow rivulets down her face.

Okay. I'm sorry, he said. Come on, Julia. We can put on one of my big shirts. You can pick which one. He pulled her toward his suitcase open in the corner of the room. Julia found a shirt from the St. George marathon and they put it over their heads. Both were left with one arm imprisoned inside the shirt.

Make a hole, said Julia. Like this. She clutched Kip's knife and cut two small holes at the front below the neck, enough room for both of them to force an arm.

The shirt bunched a bit at their waists, but when they placed their arms around one another they looked like any other couple. We're all set for Halloween, said Kip. The man with two heads.

Excuse me?

He corrected, The person with two heads.

Julia pulled her hair back in a ponytail. It's not so bad, is it? I don't think it's so bad.

He scowled. I'd still prefer to be the only person in this shirt.

Julia moved toward him and the skin curved into a weak 'C.' It's fine Kip, for now.

*J*ust think how much money we'll save on clothes, said Julia, forking a piece of pineapple into her mouth. Want some? She held a piece up to Kip's mouth. He shook his head. Of course one of us is going to have to switch their work hours.

They were huddled over a round glass table with a tropical flower arrangement shooting up from its center. Fuchsia blooms and leafy spiking things, tiny yellow curled flowers that smelled of sugar. Everything in Hawaii was sweet, as if the entire island had been dipped in sugar cane syrup.

We could do mornings at your office and I could ask Dr. Thanes to switch me to third shift. None of the ICU nurses want to work evenings, even though they end up with only half the work of the day shift. Julia watched him chew his eggs Benedict. Instead of ham, the Aloha Café had added fresh swordfish. Is that good? she asked.

Kip lifted his chin noncommittally. The table where they sat was hidden behind a den of palm trees and hearty-fingered ferns, which cut the sky into slices. The breeze ruffled the napkins on their laps. She gulped the air and its saltiness. Perhaps she had pushed the Hawaiian honeymoon too much. Kip hadn't wanted to visit Hawaii or any place surrounded by water. As a child his step-father had thrown him into the deep end of the pool at the YMCA and he had sunk to the bottom. Two lifeguards yanked him from the water and tossed him on the dry tiles where he spit up Cheerios.

Kip, are you feeling all right? When he didn't respond, she concluded that he was having second thoughts. Julia followed his fork and knife slicing back and forth on the white dish, scooping a piece of hollandaise-coated egg into his mouth.

She looked around at the other tables. There were so many beautiful women—blondes and brunettes, most wearing only bathing suits with fringed wraps around their waists. Julia wondered if Kip wished he were still a bachelor vacationing in this tropical paradise by himself. She was being foolish, she realized. Miracles didn't happen every day.

Finally he spoke up, his voice neatly pinched. Julia, the thing you've forgotten is we aren't going to stay this way. I'm still going to work at Coopers and Masterson by myself and you'll keep your day shift at the hospital. Whatever this is—he motioned at the skin—it'll wear off.

Julia used a hand to shield her eyes from the sun. She squinted and watched the gulls looping overhead.

He clapped his hands together. So let's put the idea out of our minds. Let's get into our bathing suits and work on those tans. The rays on the hotel roof will be strong.

We're in Hawaii, said Julia. We have to go to the beach. You'll be fine. No water, just sand.

I'm not fooling, Julia. If you so much as splash me, I'm on the roof.

Aye aye, captain. She saluted him. Anyways, I'm not going anywhere without you at my side and vice versa.

Oh, I don't know about that, he said. You'd find a way to get what you wanted.

Who me? She pouted. I'm as innocent as they come.

Sure, Ms. Innocent.

She grinned. That's Mrs. now.

*T*he beach spanned every direction. Multicolored umbrellas shot up from the crystalline whiteness, reclining canvas chairs were stacked in front of the Hotel Watiki and piles of fat towels stood on carts every few feet. White pillars of foam smashed the fine mounds of sand like the beat of a metronome. They set their belongings on two chaise lounges. Julia pulled off her side of their shared shirt and Kip yanked the rest off his shoulders.

She wore her red bikini with tiny bow ties at the hips. Wow. You look fantastic, Kip said. He squirted sun block onto his hands and told her to turn around.

Julia stepped out and tried to turn her back to him. Whoa. She stumbled and he caught her elbow. Thanks, she said. How do we do this?

Watch me. Kip distributed the lotion between both of his palms. He crooked his arms behind him and slapped the white cream on his back. You're going to have to do this solo, babe.

She squirted lotion into her hands and coated her arms and neck. She stopped before moving onto her legs. Kip, would you please? As if he could read her mind, he bowed at the waist and smoothed the lotion on her legs. She decided to skip her back altogether.

They pushed two of the hotel beach chairs together and Julia opened up her mystery novel, but couldn't keep her eyes on the page. Her attention drifted to the surf where two women in their early twenties frolicked in knee-deep water. They were both wearing bikinis skimpier than Julia's and their backsides were firm, like waxed blocks of cheese. They were staring at Kip.

Women were often attracted to him. He ran twelve miles a day and lifted weights for fifty-minute stretches. His dark wavy hair contrasted with his fairness, drawing out the lines of his jaw, the width of his neck. He had a wholesome, honest look to his face and even when he was in his nineties, Kip would still look young. Julia wasn't as disciplined as him. The gym bored her with its endless repetitions and blaring pop songs. She had nice hair, and Kip had once divulged it had been her long locks that initially caught his eye.

She trusted him, yet while her eyes followed the two bikini-clad women, she couldn't resist contemplating that as an attached couple Kip would be unable to have an affair. Maybe he'd been considering it and the fates interceded, fastened him to her side so he would never stray. Julia wasn't naïve. She knew he looked at other women, probably dreamed about them as well, though, ultimately, he had chosen her from the whole lot.

He was hers now.

Julia reached over and massaged Kip's thigh. She moved her hand farther up his leg. His head slanted toward her, his lips curling devilishly.

Julia woke from their nap in the honeymoon suite shrieking in pain. Kip had his pocketknife open and was making tiny scissoring cuts on the bottom of their attached skin. He leaned on his elbow while blood oozed on the sheets. She punched his arm and he dropped the knife on the bed, blade extended. What are you doing? she asked. Julia gritted her teeth and used the sheet to tie a tourniquet around the gushing skin. It felt like she'd been stabbed repeatedly with an ice pick. Darn it! She hollered, opening and closing her fists, punching the mattress. That could kill us. We could bleed to death. She focused on his face, noticed tears shimmering in his eyes.

Be tough, he said. Our options are limited. I'm not spending two weeks on vacation connected to you. No offense.

She snorted, held tight to the wounded flesh and its quickly dampening sheet. None taken. We can see a specialist if you want— you know, the guy in the phone book that separates bodies on a sliding scale. Julia pushed out of the bed and onto her feet, yanking Kip up as well.

Calm down, Julia. I just don't know how much longer I can deal with this.

Let's just get it fixed. She pulled as far away from him as she could. Let's get this whole thing annulled. You never wanted to marry me in the first place. She paused and listened to the reverberation of her words. Julia tapped the middle of her chest with her palm. She bellowed, What's so horrible about being attached to me?

Honey, listen. Kip stepped toward her until his body faced hers, like the folding in of an accordion. Let's get cleaned up and go on one of those sunset cruises—the one with all the seafood the travel agent told us about. We're both a little stressed. Let's do something relaxing. You love the water. We'll spend some time right on top of it and tomorrow morning we'll go to the hospital, see if anyone there can help us.

Julia crossed her arms and her mouth capsized into a tiny frown. He placed an arm around her back and kissed her cheek, briefly.

*J*ulia knew she wasn't faultless. While initially their lengthy engagement made her doubt his feelings for her, now she had visible proof they were supposed to be together. First, Kip wanted to wait to marry until he finished graduate school. Then, he wanted to be firmly entrenched in his job at Coopers and Masterson where he worked as an investment consultant. Then he told Julia that he wanted to save for a down payment on a house prior to becoming engaged—have you seen the interest rates out there? he had said. She had waited a long, long while for Kip and she was certain she knew him better than herself. His bachelor phase was in the past; she knew he yearned for the security of a family, just like she did, although he surprised her. What if they had a child someday and he was born with three feet—would Kip try to chop off one of those? Would he pay someone to swap a normal baby for theirs? Whatever happened brought with it a reason, yet it was not for them to judge. The flesh between them was scabbing but warm. It grew out of them equally, and Julia found herself touching the length of it, stroking the damp and pinkish swaddled flesh up and down.

*J*ulia put on a gold sequined halter dress that created circular prisms on the wall. She made an incision of five inches along the seam and zipped the dress up her side, then helped Kip get into his jacket. In the bathroom, she painted her eyelashes with mascara while he coated his face with shaving cream. As she rimmed her lips with liner, one hand absently wandered over to touch the skin peeking out from her dress and the side of Kip's suit jacket. She'd affixed five Band-Aids to cover the cut and hoped it wouldn't bleed anymore. Hey Kip, do you believe some things are predetermined?

Kip turned the faucet on hot and rinsed his disposable razor, steam clouding the lower half of the mirror. He made one long stroke along the left side of his face and turned to Julia. He put his hands on her hips and turned her so she faced him. Julia, I love you. Yes, I think we're supposed to be a couple. You're my soul mate and I'm yours. He squeezed one of her shoulders, then turned back to the mirror.

I wasn't talking about us, she said. I'm curious if particular decisions were made years ago—before we were even born. I mean, were we fated to go on this dinner cruise?

The travel agent spoke pretty highly of it, said Kip.

I know, but we hadn't made definitive plans, yet here we are.

Don't you want to go? asked Kip. I thought this would be a nice evening for us.

I'm not saying that, said Julia. I'm just thinking about how we make decisions—*if* we make them.

Hey, is there anyone else on honeymoon with you? Kip raised his eyebrows. I didn't think so. We do everything in the here and now. Except for this thing. They both looked at the skin. Who knows what this is.

Her mouth puckered.

*F*rom the start she'd known Kip was meant to be a part of her life. He was the first to ask questions about her work at the hospital and had even encouraged her to enroll in graduate classes. Surely this new addition to their bodies held an equally important function.

Julia hooked an arm around his back and crossed the other arm in front of her middle so she could fix her hand on the flesh. It reminded her of pajamas she'd worn as a girl that had a tiny opening below the belly button. She often pretended while wearing them that she was a kangaroo and it was the pouch for her young.

They took the glass elevator to the hotel lobby and agreed to walk the half-mile to the S.S. Emperor, a gleaming pewter ship half the size of a city block. Kip and Julia walked with their arms around one another. Traffic was heavy as locals zipped home from offices, windows rolled down, their hair flapping into wings. Stores blinked to life. Souvenir shops displayed postcards and the jewelers had diamond conch earrings presented on red pillows, while a darkly-lit piano bar advertised fresh coconut cream pie.

Julia stopped in front of a storefront displaying a spectacular gown of navy silk with rhinestone-tipped straps. It sparkled under two hanging spotlights. She could almost feel the soft, light drape of the fabric. She glanced beyond the window where two saleswomen folded scarves in front of a table. She couldn't just force Kip in a dressing room with her, not yet. That would take time. They would have years to become accustomed to their shared flesh. Their kids would play London bridges beneath their attachment and try and swing on it as if it were a monkey bar. When they were old and retired, they'd help each other. No need for a walker. Even as seniors they'd share a king-sized bed, no cold, twin-sized beds for them.

Come on, said Kip, pulling at her midsection.

Julia glanced at the dress shop's hours for future reference. As they walked on, an outdoor café played a song by the Cars while waiters in red aprons served sandwiches on oversized platters. The movie theater's flashing marquee garishly illuminated the street. At the corner, a man played a polka on a violin the size of a cantaloupe. Kip tossed a dollar into his tattered case.

As they walked the gangplank of the S.S. Emperor, honking horns and music from the open-aired eateries faded. Kip stopped mid-stride on the gangplank, held tight to the railing, gulped.

You okay? asked Julia. We're almost there. Waves licked the

sides of the ship, but it remained steady. She reached over and took his halting hand in hers. It's going to be just fine. He nodded and they continued walking. Flags from every nation flapped above the deck and tiny white lights twinkled on the railings. The inside of the S.S. Emperor was carpeted in a plush wine color. Oil paintings dressed the walls and gold brocade draperies hung from the ballroom windows. A bald man in a finely-creased tuxedo seated them near two open glass doors.

The chairs were velour, dressed in the same shade as the carpet. The maître d' held out a chair for Julia. She crouched halfway in the seat, careful not to sit, while Kip dragged his chair beside hers. She sunk into the rich fabric.

Kip grabbed the shared flesh. Damn!

Ouch! yelled Julia. She jerked up and both of them rubbed their joined skin. Sorry, said Julia, I thought you were already sitting. They both leaned forward in their seats, their skin rested taut across the arms of the chairs. She grimaced, tapped the flesh with her fingertips. This isn't too comfortable.

Hey, I don't feel much better, said Kip. Only a few more hours. Tomorrow we'll leave for the hospital.

Julia furrowed her brows. Let's not talk about that now. She would make a believer of him yet. She scanned the room. This is amazing, she said.

They're supposed to have the world's largest seafood buffet, he said. He knocked the top of the table. A little discomfort won't be the end of us. Let's get the grub.

They walked up and down the table that lined half of the ballroom wall. One-half of the table was heaped with ice sculptures and the other displayed red meats beneath heat lamps. After they both filled tiny plates with shrimp, Julia announced that she wanted to move onto the deck to catch the last glimmer of sun.

Kip hovered at their table and looked out at the water.

Julia took his hand and led him to the ship's prow, underneath an American flag that snapped at attention. They kept their arms around each other. Julia dipped one of the jumbo shellfish into a pool of red sauce and Kip did the same; they crossed arms at the elbows, feeding one another. He ate his in one bite while she finished hers in three nibbles. You pig! she mocked. He snorted. They laughed. The band started a waltz, the music floating out to them. Their faces were lit in a burnished rosy color.

Taking the fragile silver-rimmed plate from her hands, he asked her to dance. They dropped their arms from each other's waists and the shared skin bent like a drawn bow. She leaned in to rest her cheek against his and he ran a hand down her bare back, relaxing it above the concave of her spine. She swayed to the music. Despite the wind skimming off the ocean, Julia felt comfortable. She concentrated on her steps and opened her eyes to glance at her feet. Rhythm had always been something she lacked. Kip was the one who seemed to naturally know how to move. She nuzzled him, breathed the spicy smell of his shaving cream and looked out at the ocean.

This is when she caught sight of the raft.

It was small and made of rubber, and nearly as black as the water. Tiny splashes along the sides made it clear where the raft ended and the water began. Someone, something was inside. Julia called out, waved her hands overhead, and received no response. A sharp pain suddenly welled in her side, in the place where the new flesh had grown. The pain was as vicious as what she'd experienced that afternoon when Kip had attempted to cut them apart. Julia understood. The purpose for their extended bodies was floating in the Pacific, right in front of her.

Kip looked up at her. She yanked him over to the side of the boat. She grabbed the rail and tried to pull herself up. A woman behind them screamed and pointed at the water.

Kip's weight held her firmly on the deck. Jesus! Are you crazy?

This is—she spoke slowly—the reason for our attachment. We need to help whoever that is out there.

Where? In there? I don't swim. Julia. I'm not going in there.

She pulled him closer to the barrier and placed one hand on the uppermost handrail. Now we are each going to put our knees right up there. She pointed to the top rail.

I'm not doing it, said Kip.

Yes, you are. I won't let anything happen to you. Julia positioned an arm around his shoulders. She threw her weight forward and pulled him in front of the railings. One knee, Kip. Right there. She patted the barrier's chill metal.

Oh no. No. Jul—

The rest happened quickly. Julia was no diver, but she was naturally strong. She flung her arms overhead and leapt off the S.S. Emperor, pulling Kip overboard with her. The water was bitter, icy. Her blood instantly cooled. The salt blurred her eyes. She could only see black, could only feel biting blackness. He was heavy beside her, weighing her down. Kicking her feet in a dumb scissor, it felt as if her legs were separated from the rest of her. She touched the flesh between them with her hand; it seemed shriveled and plastic, nothing real, nothing that lived and breathed with them. Just as quickly, she recalled her purpose. She cupped her hands and vigorously kicked her feet. First, she felt the bubbles against her legs, then noticed her hair draping downwards. They were moving up, toward the surface. Popping out of the water like corks, they gasped. Water spurted out of their noses. Kip grabbed Julia around the waist. The dim light of the moon glinted off wave caps lighting the water; she could see the raft better now, and as she kept them afloat she noticed the child slumped on his back. His hair was dark and his lips white and scaly. His skin was the color of a nectarine, blistered and puffed.

Julia used a butterfly kick and held onto Kip, propping his head above the water. The ship's sirens screamed. There was splashing behind them and without looking back, Julia was certain they were tossing life preservers into the water. Someone yelled, Hang on!

She brought them over to the side of the raft where they grabbed hold. The boy looked about six years old. Several empty jugs and candy wrappers rolled at his feet. They dragged themselves into the raft and it heaved, rode the waves, rolling up and up, pummeling down, crashing back in the smooth underbelly of a wave before being raked up again. Julia held a hand over her mouth. She could taste the shrimp making a quick reappearance. A hollow plop dropped in the water farther off and she looked up to see a wooden boat from the S.S. Emperor trolling in the direction of the raft.

The boy's eyes fluttered. He opened his mouth but no sound came. We're going to help you, she said. She took the boy's pulse using Kip's watch. It was faint. She ripped his raggedy undershirt and held a palm full of water to his burning forehead. Julia used both of her hands to examine the boy's tiny arms and legs. She pressed his middle and palpitated his sides, watched the boy's face. We've got to get him to a hospital. He's badly dehydrated.

The little boy fixed on the bluish flesh uniting Julia and Kip. He murmured something incomprehensible. What'd he say? asked Kip. The boy slowly moved onto his knees, his face contorted by the change of position. He bent body over knees, his vertebrae protruded like eggs, ribs distinct parallel fissures. He placed his hands together and the skin crackled, as dry as two bones rubbed together. He bowed in front of Julia, his voice was papery, frail, *Mama*, he said. He bowed again, tapping his pressed hands in the air. *Mama.*

Julia put her hand on the boy's head. Peace, she said.

The boy crawled toward her knees, continued to bow in front of her, stopping only to glance at the joined flesh. He unclasped his hands and reached out, placed one hand in the middle of the skin.

Kip trembled, pulled his torso away from the boy's touch. Keep your hands to yourself, he shouted. Turning to Julia, he said, He thinks we're freaks.

He's a child. She moved deliberately, grasped the boy's wrist and directed it to the skin. Go on, she told him. It's okay. Julia kept her hand on top of the boy's and guided it back and forth. That's nice, she said, smiling. Thank you.

The boy kept his hand on the skin until Julia gently pushed him by his shoulders into the middle of the raft. She leaned over the side, tugging Kip with her. She put her hands in the black water and began paddling.

That isn't going to help, said Kip. The boat's right there. Kip leaned back as much as he could and watched its approach. The wooden boat motored and bobbed before them. She continued to paddle, even after the rescue boat had tossed a rope and Kip had caught it.

A man in a yellow jacket shouted to them.

Julia continued paddling and paused only to yell out: This boy needs immediate medical attention.

Kip stuck his hand in the water and grabbed Julia's wet fingers and she lifted her head to see where they were.

*T*he emergency room physicians at St. Andrew's Hospital

wanted to examine Julia and Kip, but the couple refused. We're sturdy stock, thanks anyways, said Kip. They kept their arms around each other. Her lower back warmed beneath his arm until it felt like it was baking. He directed them toward the red-lit exit sign and whispered into her ear, Take it slow and steady.

We aren't going anywhere without that boy. *He* is the reason. She motioned at their shared flesh.

He looked at her blankly. Blinked.

That boy is the reason our bodies grew together, she said. We were supposed to save him and now we're going to raise him and give him all the love we've got.

He chuckled. Cleared his throat. Be serious. Listen to yourself. He elongated each syllable. That boy has a family of his own just like you and I are a family. He should be with them.

He's already ours, said Julia.

We've got other things to deal with right now. Kip swatted the flesh. We aren't ready to adopt and we're in a *hospital*. It's like bank robbers returning to the savings and loan. It's not safe.

What greater proof do you need? Julia stopped, halting him as well. I won't go another step.

I could carry you, said Kip.

I'll scream. I'll show them the flesh. They can have my half.

The hospital floors were waxed. Someone's footsteps beyond them squeaked like tires on wet pavement. Kip's arm fell from Julia and her arm fell from him until their hands hung at their sides. Her arm felt bare, ill at ease on its own, dangling from her shoulders. Her fingers, drawn by the sudden coldness, feebly reached out for the flesh between them; she stroked its solidness and tried to gather her thoughts. Maybe the flesh was growing. With the right nutrients, vitamins, and exercise, the skin that attached them might expand even farther. Maybe they'd wake up in two years to find they shared one leg or one arm. How would Kip handle that? Her breath caught as she considered the miraculousness of it all—he'd never appreciate it. Her head swirled. Maybe with time she and the boy and the other children that would seek them out could teach him.

The hospital intercom paged various doctors. Staff members in pastel-colored scrubs sped past, urging gurneys of medicines and linens. Orderlies pushed wheelchairs with newly-admitted patients, while Julia and Kip stood in the hallway, leaning against the pale green walls. Julia fixed on the automatic doors that huffed open, emitting the balmy night. She waited for Kip to say something; she listened closely. Julia only heard his breathing and thought it sounded much like her own.

# Scar Serum

"Lorna, do you know how many kids in this country gash open their skin every day? Billions. Look here." Mr. Carpone pointed to a space above his right cheekbone and angled his face in the light over the worktable. "Feel it." Taking my hand, he traced a scar that stretched from his hairline into the middle of his cheek. "I got that when I fell off my bike—I was a boy, then."

I looked closer, delighted to know about the scar, an incident that occurred years before I became his assistant.

Mr. Carpone picked up a small brown glass bottle and swirled its contents with a rubber dropper. "Watch." He opened the blade of a pocketknife and made a quick stab on his forearm. Blood appeared in a slim crevice. Mr. Carpone wiped the red away and I could see the faint indentation he'd made. He dabbed a few drops of the scar serum on his arm and the beads of blood hung suspended in the fluid. When he rubbed it into the cut, new bits of skin filled in the open space. Within minutes, Mr. Carpone's arm was healed—no cut, no scar. It was as if the blade had never touched his arm. "Now you," he said.

I held up my hands in protest and began to sweat. Mr. Carpone tipped his head to the side and smiled lightly then asked, "Where's Mom today?"

His question reminded me that he was all I had. I straightened up. "Auditioning for some cleaning commercial. She's probably leaning over someone else's toilet right now, using every bit of elbow grease she has."

"It won't always be this way," he said. "Not if I can help it."

"Our bathroom is never clean," I told him. "She spends all her time impressing a bunch of executives with her disinfecting techniques." He clicked his tongue and in that pointed sound I felt redeemed.

He waved the bottle of scar serum and I took two steps backwards. "Come on, Lorna. You're my assistant. And you're brave." Yes, I was, on both counts. So I rolled up the sleeve of my T-shirt. While most of the other girls in my class were shopping at The Limited and wearing colorful, fuzzy sweaters, I chose to spend my afternoons in Mr. Carpone's basement. I closed my eyes. Upstairs I could hear the music that signaled the end of *General Hospital*. Next, Mrs. Carpone would watch *Jeopardy* with Alex Trebeck, who she found handsome. Once, she told me I should marry a man with hands like his—she said they would take me places.

I didn't care about anyone else's hands. Only Mr. Carpone's beautiful fingers spoke to me in a way I understood.

Sharp pain stung my neck and I opened my eyes. Mr. Carpone stood with the blade in hand—blood tinged its end. He held a paper towel below my jaw. "We've already done my arm. I needed to try a different section. You'll be fine." His hand steadied my shoulder. I swallowed. The truth was I would let Mr. Carpone do whatever he wanted. He'd chosen me.

Nothing he did to me could hurt much.

When he took off the towel, bits of it stuck to my skin and Mr. Carpone had to scrape it with his fingernails. I watched in a square of mirror as he applied the serum and the skin made over. He took my face in his hands and turned it to the left and right and said, "It's beautiful. Not a mark."

If only the rest of my life could be made over so easily.

I had spent the last few days eating my lunch in the handicapped stall at school. Earlier that summer, the girl I considered my best friend moved away. So now when I walked down the hall and my classmates mimicked the sound of thunder or mooed like cows, I didn't have anyone to pretend to be in deep conversation with. But at Mr. Carpone's, none of that mattered. Here, I was vital to the success of his project. He needed me.

Initially Mom had asked the Carpones to keep an eye on me while she secretly went to auditions, and after a while, I began to go there without being told to do so.

After the first night Mr. Carpone tried his scar serum on me, Mom served tuna casserole and a green salad. She filled my plate three-fourths salad and one measly spoonful of the creamy noodles. "You aren't that hungry, are you?" she asked while I held my plate suspended. She turned to my father. "I read in the paper today they're holding auditions for the musical *Annie*. Wouldn't that be great for Lorna?" A folded-over copy of *Business Week* sat beside my father's glass of wine. She cleared her throat and tapped a fingernail on the rim of his plate. "Charles, wouldn't an extracurricular be great?"

"If that's what Lorna wants."

It wasn't the enthusiasm Mom had hoped for and the discussion came to a screeching halt. Dad thought theatrics were foolish. If it had been up to him, my mom and I would both be volunteers at the cancer center, just like the spouses and daughters of the other attorneys. As if she was auditioning for another part, Mom abruptly pushed back her chair. She stormed into the kitchen where she dialed the phone number of her best friend and the two of them would spend the next few hours reliving their starring roles.

Meanwhile, I went upstairs to my room. I was halfway through a biography of a bag lady and was hoping to finish it by the weekend. The truth was I had no interest in being on stage, my form illuminated in the cape of lights. I preferred books and my room to uncertain spaces. While I was reading, there was a knock on my door and Mom burst in, flopping on my bed like some love-torn teenager. Her eyes were dry and she squealed, pounded the quilt with her fist. She shook the book in my hand. "I got the part! I'm going to be the Mighty Scrub Mom!" I congratulated her and shifted my weight, plopped a pillow on its side and leaned on it. "You can't tell your father. I'm going to share the good news when the time is right." She patted my ankle. "What do you think he'll say?" I didn't have the slightest clue. She continued, "He's used to having me to himself. But he's going to have to share me. In the commercial—Lorna, are you listening?"

I held my thumb on the page I had been reading and looked up at her.

"In the first scene, I've just finished washing dishes and I'm scouring the sink. We've had spaghetti for dinner, though, and I simply cannot get the sink clean. I've been leaning over it for half the night when Captain Mighty Scrub arrives with his scrubbing fleet and helps me get the job done in a flash." She snapped her fingers.

"It sounds good," I told her.

"Good? This is just the beginning. Maybe someday you'll want to follow in your mom's footsteps."

Perhaps I should have told her then that I was Mr. Carpone's assistant and that someday the two of us would share a home. At night, I would make Mr. Carpone dinner and together, we would eat as much as we wanted.

Mom spoke louder. "What are you reading?" I showed her the cover. "Huh. I never read that one." She pecked the air near my cheek and skittered away, leaving the door wide open.

That night, I dreamed of being chased by rivers of blood, curling brooks bubbling with my own life force, endless rivulets pouring out of vast orifices on my body. I was a fountain moored in the ground. While the blood spread out of me, Mr. Carpone remained at my side, advising me. In the dream I held his hand and it covered my own completely.

I woke with a pillow guarding my chest.

The next day, Mom told me she had arranged for me to take the bus to and from school, and that it would only be for a little while during the filming of the Mighty Scrub commercial.

"But this is just between us. To your father and anyone else who asks, I'm volunteering for hospice."

This didn't make any sense to me. "What about when the commercial airs? Dad will find out at some point."

"Watch your mouth, miss."

"I was just wondering," I said.

"Well, don't." She pinched my cheek and then glanced down at my second bowl of Choco Flakes. I pretended not to notice.

When the bus dropped me off on our street that afternoon, I went directly to the Carpone's house. "You are a smart cookie," said Mr. Carpone. We were in his basement workshop and I was sitting on the stool where he usually sat. I had told him my idea for a scar serum commercial. In it, two neighborhood kids collide on bikes. The two boys do not know each other because one has recently moved into the neighborhood. They go back to one of the boy's homes and apply the serum, and by the end of the commercial they ride off toward an ice cream truck. "You're too intelligent for the kids your age, aren't you? That's why you're my assistant."

I felt myself blush. I couldn't tell him that in my dreams there were only the two of us and that sometimes the blood would not stop.

"And we'll ask your mom to star in the commercial, right?" He chuckled. "No, no. You'll always be the star here." Truthfully, I didn't even want him to mention my parents. At his house, I only wanted him to consider me.

"We're going to do our legs today, Lorna love. It's got to be done."

I had momentarily forgotten the work, our purpose. I nodded. Refocused.

He reminded me, "When we send the papers for the trademark we've got to make sure everything's been accounted for. Then we'll get you your money." I didn't have any clue what I'd do with my share of the earnings, although Mr. Carpone had said we'd be wealthy and that my college tuition would be paid.

He turned his back while I unzipped my pants. I pretended we were two lovers who lived in a homeless shelter like in the book I was reading. My pants hung at my ankles. I looked away when Mr. Carpone opened up the knife. My underpants were white and generous.

The cut was on the meat of my thigh, long and thin like a sliver of paper and I yelped like a puppy, something to be pitied. Mr. Carpone pressed a clean paper towel against it, the blood a quick streak of red. "They'll want to know we've tested this in every possible situation." He dabbed on the serum. It felt like chilled olive oil as he kneaded it into my thigh.

Mr. Carpone's hands were remarkably tender, as if they were filled with jam. As he rubbed, he talked. "If I had a daughter like you I wouldn't leave you with the neighbors." He shook his head. "You deserve only the best. And someday your parents will come to your mansion and you will decide whether or not to open the front door, right?"

Our mansion, I wanted to say. The one we owned equally, decorated with the awards our scar serum would win.

He pulled back his hands and we both leaned in. Skin had filled in the cut without a blemish. "You know, when I was your age the only school subject I understood was science. So I read every scientific book I could get my hands on. Everyone thought I was a fool, except for Mrs. Carpone. She said I'd be a scientist and look, I am."

A tiny lump fixed itself in my stomach. Mrs. Carpone wasn't his assistant—I'd never even seen her downstairs. I told him: "My mother thinks I could be a model if I lost weight."

"Poor Lorna," said Mr. Carpone. "Poor lovely Lorna." He touched my cheek. "You will always be my brilliant assistant. Always the best."

*L*ater that evening, I leaned against the couch where my father read the newspaper and I read my book. I became angry when in my book, the bag lady had a cough and she had to wait in line for a whole day until a doctor at the clinic could see her. The unfairness of it all. Mom had told Dad she was volunteering for the local hospice organization. Really, she was auditioning for a part in a soap opera—*Hours of Our Day*—and the thought of real patients on soiled sheets, waiting for death to relieve them only added to my fury. We were waiting to eat dinner with her. "When will Mom be back?" I asked him.

"I don't know exactly. When she's done."

He was so unaware. "What does a hospice volunteer do?" I asked.

"You'll have to ask your mother." He flipped a page, and then stood up, holding his empty wine glass. He headed for the liquor cabinet.

"You think she helps them?" I asked.

"Who? Oh yes," he said. He uncorked the bottle of wine, refilled his glass. I didn't understand my parents' marriage or even the Carpone's, for that matter. Why did they remain together when it was obvious that the whole lot of them were better off alone? Except for Mr. Carpone. He should be with me.

"Why are you still married to Mom?"

Dad sighed. "Lorna, you know this. We love each other."

"How do you know?" I asked.

"We had you, didn't we?" He flipped to another section of newspaper.

I asked, "Do you think she loves you?"

"Lorna, I'm tired."

"I need to know," I continued. "What would end it for you?"

*I*n my room, I tore off my clothes, piled them into a heap, and got into bed. The sheets were smooth against my bare skin. I closed my eyes and pretended Mr. Carpone was with me. He would pat my shoulder, his handprint warm and steady before he told me where he needed to try out the serum. I would undo the laces on my gym shoes and slide off my jeans without being asked.

"Lovely Lorna," he would sigh. I would undo the buttons of my shirt, and stand there, hair hanging in my face, the beginner's bra conforming to the mounds on my chest. He would take off his shirt as well, rubbing my arms.

The light would bounce off his scalp. Smelling of limes, he would make tiny scissoring cuts on every stretch of skin from my neck to my feet. After each slash he'd cry out, dab at the wound with the towel and ask, "That's not so bad, Lorna, is it?" His eyes brimming with tears, his other hand already reaching for the bottle so he could put me back together. "It hurts me more," he'd murmur.

I would pray his steady hands might slip, that the knife would pierce deeper, dive into a warm place where only a prick of blood would mark the entry way and the point might pierce through to the other side. Finally, he would hand me the blade. Still wet with my blood, its pearl handle smooth, he would instruct, "Go on, I'm ready." But first I would kiss him hard—on the lips. And he'd kiss me back. "Oh Lorna," he'd say. And I would open my arms to him.

From downstairs, I heard my mother's voice calling me, and all too suddenly, I remembered who I was.

*O*ver fajitas, Mom told us about a woman with a brain tumor she had met at hospice. "She has such spirit! She's only in her fifties, but she has an amazing outlook on life. Today I read her some of the New Testament and she was very grateful." I peeled back the warm tortilla on my fajita. It held a tablespoon of meat.

"She sounds tough," said my father.

Mom's lies were exhausting. I finished my fajita first, my plate marred only by a spot of orange grease. This was no place for Mr. Carpone's brilliant assistant.

Like any good actress, I became poised, found my center. "Dad, did you know Mom's the new Mighty Scrub lady?" I tilted my head toward my audience and projected my voice. "She's going to be famous—isn't that great?"

*I* fumed upstairs, my parents' voices crossed over one another, canceling out the clarity of a single word. Finally. They would go their separate ways and I would too. I packed a bag, put on my pajamas, and slipped under the blankets. Their words sounded like flags snapping in the wind. After a few hours, when the voices fell to a hush, Mom entered my room.

"I still love you, honey. It's going to be all right." I shivered, clasped my arms tight. "I forgive you," she said. Yet I felt the same—black, heavy. Filled with something immobile.

After hours of blinking into the darkness, I took my bag and left for the Carpone's. The sky was cloaked in dark folds and our street numbed of sound. I crouched beside their bedroom window where the faint light illuminated their forms. Mrs. Carpone was dressed in a long white gown and she sat across from her shirtless husband, his arm cradled in hers. She held a kitchen knife in her palm and they were both grinning. I pounded on the window as hard as I could and their faces jolted, squinted at my oily locks and round face. Who else could it be? Mr. Carpone's eyes narrowed in on mine, daring me to keep quiet, but it was too late for silence. I had come to be with him.

I slammed the pillar of my wrist against the window, into my own glimmering reflection. My arm crashed through the glass, shards stabbing my skin. Real blood. It ran fast, streaking down my arm and onto the Carpone's beige carpeting. It was darker than ever as if it was drawing from the deepest part of me, a place that I recently discovered, a place that craved revenge.

# The Memory Woman

**W**e go to the memory woman because one of us has received a gerbil for his birthday. We wonder what the gerbil is thinking. The memory woman says the little creature is heartbroken and that she dreams of her playmate and friend. The memory woman stretches her hand out across the trees. You should let her go, she says, you don't want to be responsible for sorrow. We listen to her, let the gerbil scurry from our hands, watch it dash along the underbrush.

We can see her house with its blue silky curtains on our way from school if we bow behind the trunks of the paper birches, although we aren't supposed to go near where she lives. Anissa says that the memory woman once made soup from a man's hand because he lied to her. This is what Anissa's older brother has told her. We aren't certain if we believe this. Our parents tell us to leave the memory woman alone. Let her be, they say. She is old. She has always lived in that house on that hill. We will be grounded if they find that we have not started our chores and that we dawdle in the woods.

She likes it when we bring her yellow apples, wrapped packages of peanut butter and crackers, mini chocolate bars ribboned with caramel that she grabs, tucks into the pockets of her crocheted shawl. We press our small hands to her knotted ones and hope some of her powers will rub off on us.

We believe that she was born in the sea and that her mother was a gull and her father a sparkly fish that leapt into the air to greet his wife with a kiss. We are sure deep water granted her the power to read memories.

Before we go home to start our chores, we reenact the beginning of time when the lands were covered in low bushes and our parents did not yet stand over us, hands thrashing through hair. Our cave is hidden in outcroppings between the rocks. We pair up boy-girl, husband-wife. We rub sticks together, puff our cheeks with air, and blow. We are always close to starting a fire. We draw sticks, just like those that were there at the beginning, and choose the one to be the animal. The person playing the animal must walk on his hands and knees and howl when our husbands stab him with invisible spears, searing his heart. He rolls onto his back, shakes, and dies. The husbands drag him and then drop him at our feet where we prepare his meat into stew.

After we have finished our chores, we regroup at the gully; it is here where we see the gold tape flapping on the beach. We cut through sea grass prickling our legs, stick our arms out like airplanes, and kick up sand. Clouds spin past our fluttering fingers as we head toward the red and blue flashing lights.

Uniformed adults stand in clumps. We crouch down, push past the men that have finished their shift at the cannery. There are two bloated bodies, girls, clasped hands loosened, puffed white with purple and green marks along their backsides. They have swollen bellies and knotted tresses. The girls are covered with a black tarp, thick and weighted so we can only see the dull outline of their shapes.

An hour later we're on the hill. It's the memory woman who tells us how the water transformed their bodies, two sisters submerged. For the first time, we do not need to ask her questions. She tells us how they dove into the waves, right off the jagged rocks, thrilled by the crashing sounds; the spray dotted their bare thighs and they spun, twirled in the water, joining hands high above their heads. The sea said, Stay with me, and danced pirouettes with their bony ankles. The waves tried to chase the girls, tickling them with splash, nudging them toward our shore. The memory woman says they were giggling as the water tossed them about. When Anissa asks, the memory woman says that they felt no pain and that the colors marking their skin were part of a game.

We believe her, hand her a package of fudge-striped cookies for the memory. But the memory woman shakes her head, will not accept our gift, says, I am tired, and then turns back inside her house. Anissa thinks maybe the memory woman misses her sister. This is news to us. We didn't know she had a sister. Anissa says she's not certain.

We talk about the two sisters they found in the water when the sun bends low over the incoming tide and our faces become the color of mangoes. We take each other's hands and jump into the air, holding our breath, while one of the boys pretends he is the sea and tosses pebbles at our backs.

# Madera Bree

Miles from Madera Bree's land, the smell of pigs curdled the air. They strolled the acres of her property and each time she stepped outside they squealed, high and roping in three strong syllables: Wee oo oo! Wee oo oo! Wee oo oo! No one who heard the pigs denied that it sounded like, We love you! And it was good that the pigs loved Madera Bree, for others were not nice to her.

According to the best calculations, Madera Bree was over three hundred and forty years old, and still her shoulders and arms flaunted firm ripples. She ran ten miles a day around her property with only a powdery sweat dotting her upper lip. Her dark hair was long and fell down her back in a careless sheen like the endless hum of Beaver Creek rolling through the center of town. Madera Bree could have easily passed for a high school senior, a girl on the fringe of womanhood, yet all her friends had died. She could scarcely recall the faces of her family and she was haunted with the reality that she would be called to bear witness to life's evolutions again and again.

She could not withstand much more heartache.

Since she refused to share her secret for longevity, most of the community believed she did not deserve to have it. In the year 2000, a cash reward was offered to whoever could age Madera Bree. Ten thousand dollars. Jack Levers was confident he could win the prize.

Unemployment in Beaver County had reached an all-time high. Men were forced to take part-time jobs in nearby communities, driving one or two hours each way to work as mechanics or maintenance workers at the golf courses. When word of the ten thousand dollar reward became widespread, there was talk about what one could do with that amount of money. Most of the people at the Schoolhouse Tavern had very clear ideas for how they'd spend it.

"Me and the wife would get a sitter and we'd fly to Vegas," said Tucker, tipping back his bottle of beer.

"Sure, and then the money'd be gone before it had a chance to even get warm in your pocket," quipped Sadie as she moved back and forth behind the bar.

"Shoot, Sadie. You sound as bad as my wife."

"That's right, 'cause I know what Louise would do with that kind of cash and I guarantee it wouldn't involve any blackjack."

Burt, who grew corn, added his two cents. "I'd take you all out for pork tenderloin."

"You would not," retorted Jack Levers. "You're a selfish jerk like the rest of us." A fair-skinned bachelor, Jack Levers had dimples and a trimmed, copper-colored beard scattered with bits of white. He claimed himself a businessman and although he was not as financially hard-strapped as the other men sitting beside him, he, too, was interested in increasing his wealth. He had already discovered through microfiche records at the *Beaver County Digest* that Madera Bree owned her house and the thirty acres it inhabited.

Baptized at St. Michael's Church, she had not attended mass since her own wedding over a hundred years ago. Most interesting to Jack Levers was the fact she regularly ordered books from the Beaver County Library on Wheels.

Sadie piped up, "Well, you're all being stupid if you ask me 'cause she ain't gonna get old—she's just a miracle living in our midst."

"She's no miracle, Sadie. She's gonna get old just like everybody else. Then she'll die. I'll make her die." Jack lifted his drink and proposed a toast. "To gray hair and wrinkles and broken hips." Tucker and Burt picked up their beers, even Sadie grabbed a Pepsi and toasted. "I bet you an additional grand I'll age her," said Jack.

"Not unless I get to her first," laughed Tucker.

Prepared to obtain her secret of longevity in any way, Jack Levers said, "Just watch me."

Madera Bree dressed in long skirts that brushed the ground, dark socks, tennis shoes with holes. She wore oxford shirts that once belonged to her husband. They were stained and torn in places, held together with safety pins or a bit of yarn, although even her dowdy clothes could not disguise her girlish shape. Her hips were narrow, waist trim and firm, supple breasts any man in town would have given his left hand to fondle. Not that any of them had the chance, for Madera Bree had lived alone too long.

Her house was camouflaged by a nest of alders and spruce at the end of a hilly plain exactly one-quarter mile from Beaver Creek's cold, gushing water. The house was multiple shades of brown and squat, a chubby-jowled urchin that looked as if it was perpetually stooping. When the town's youngsters arrived at Madera's house to take their aim at the cash reward, she was perched on the couch, selecting a story to read to her pigs.

The pack of children squatted outside her house and threw rocks against the windows; shattering glass sprayed the ground. They broke every window and then jumped up with clanging bells and whistles clamped between their teeth. Madera Bree jolted from her spot on the couch and let out a peaked cry, the squeak of an abandoned kitten. The children ran off cheering and Madera chased them a mile, then stopped to stare at their miniature forms disappearing through the ferns. She could have grabbed any number of them, but then what? Behind her was the rhythmic mewing of her pigs, Wee oo oo! Wee oo oo! Wee oo oo!

The women of Beaver County figured they had an advantage over Madera Bree, since they were women themselves. They attempted to age her by showing her horrific current events. She didn't expose herself to the rest of the world, they reasoned; of course she remained youthful. They dressed in black and stood in front of Madera Bree's house pleading with her to face reality: "Look, look!" they demanded when she cracked open her door. They held newspaper articles about malnourished children, disease, and airplanes erupting into fiery balloons, civil wars that butted brother against brother. "You can't deny this," they said, surrounding her, shaking their fists at her. "It's real!"

She pushed a maple desk in front of the door and crouched behind it, trembling. Go away, she thought. Away away away. The women ran their fingernails along the walls while goosebumps popped along Madera's arms. They crumpled the clippings and hurled them into the now windowless openings of her house. After taking a cigarette lighter to the end of a black and white photo of drought-ravished cattle, one woman threw the picture into the house. Instantly, jagged flames leapt at the two-hundred-year-old rug, dry as salt. Madera screamed. She whipped off her shoes and smacked the flames; her long hair singed and snapped as the fire whirled up around her body. Dense gray plumes rose and twisted, braided and overlapped. The wall beneath the window darkened, smoldered. She whacked at the carpeting. Smoke burned her eyes. Madera Bree choked, swatted the wall with her bare hand and dumped a moist houseplant onto the floor. Finally the smoke thinned and began to escape through the windows. The women's laughter trickled away while the reek of charred roots remained.

Madera Bree's left arm roared—it had been caught in the flames and it felt as if a million knives were piercing her forearm. She filled the sink with water and leaned into the bath, soaked the skin up to her shoulder. Outside, fireflies danced above the pigs' squiggly tails and the moon lurked low, throwing blocks of light on the dirt. Her shoulders slumped in exhaustion.

Blisters and small white patches appeared from her wrist to the lower section of Madera's elbow. An ashy splotch spread along the wall. Madera used her hip to push the couch over the black-crusted rug. She filled buckets with water and used her good arm to line them up along the inside of the house. Clutching the injured arm across her chest, she peeked out into the night, nervously blinking.

In the morning, she only ventured outdoors to tend to the pigs. She fumbled with the use of one arm, dropped the water hose repeatedly. She aimed the hose at the trough and when she turned on the nozzle, the spray drenched her tennis shoes. The pigs rallied around her, nudged her legs with their narrow heads. She turned off the water and stooped to pat their short, fuzzed hair.

She thought she saw shadows creeping along the walls, and one idea haunted her: they had returned. This time they would use axes to slice through the walls. They would grab her and take her to the middle of town, shouting and hooting, tossing their fists in the sky, only stopping once they reached the rocky banks of Beaver Creek. They would want to see if she could survive other feats as well as aging. They would count. One, two, three, and four, and strong hands would wrap around her head and neck and shove her beneath the chilled waters. In her mind it always ended with the same result: while they held her underwater she inevitably breathed and everything clouded.

Madera Bree smoothed aloe salve on her arm and bandaged it as best she could with an old T-shirt and packaging tape. She ate the food from her garden and napped on the couch, her body suddenly feverish, craving the heavy hand of sleep, the sure pushing off and sailing away. She shared the space in her lap with her injured arm. She was doing just that, eyelids drooping, on the day Jack Levers, the fair-haired bachelor, strode up the path to her house carrying a box full of books and wearing a Beaver County Library volunteer tag.

Crunching gravel alerted her to his footsteps. She jerked awake, clutched her bad arm and cowered in a corner of the kitchen farthest from the front of the house. She remained motionless. The soft pigs rambled out back. Furtively, she could slide out the window above the sink, live the life of a sow. Before she could further contemplate her options, there was a knock on the door and then a head poked inside the space where a window should have been. "Hello?" Madera hid behind the refrigerator, certain he could not see her.

"Hi, ma'am. How are you today?"

Madera jumped, moved closer to the sink. She cradled the arm in its yellowing dress, then righted her shoulders, pushed her head higher. She walked into the living room and stared at the man's tag; it said he was a volunterr for the Beaver County Library. He patted the box. "I've brought you some books. I'm Jack."

He patted the box again.

"Yes." Madera remained frozen, stood sideways away from the man.

"I'm a first-time volunteer and we're trying some new scheduling things. That's why I'm here today. We're trying to get all the books delivered on one day early in the week. That way we won't have to make so many trips."

Stories for the pigs. Madera shot forth and grabbed the box. As soon as its weight was in her hands she screamed. Books toppled onto the floor and spilled across the room.

"Oops. I'm sorry." Jack Levers pointed to the door. "Would you mind?" He didn't wait for Madera's answer, but pried into her house. "Ma'am? The door is stuck." He rammed against the entry. Wood splintered.

After gliding inside, he scanned the pails of water, stacks of books, and dusty veneer tables. The air smelled of decades of pigs as if their generous rumps and hefty bones were embedded in the furniture. Jack held his breath as he squatted down and picked up the books one by one, dropping them into the box. "Did you cut yourself?"

"This?" Madera looked down at the arm and shrugged, her voice parched, unused. She crackled, "A little burn." She moved closer to the door and rested her good arm against the desk. "Thank you for the books."

Jack flashed his infamous grin, the one women always complimented, tipped his head at her and said, "See you next week." He crossed close enough for her to smell his cologne. Returning to the van, Jack craned his neck up at the sky and held the pose as if daylight was an entirely new concept; it was the best side of his face and he wanted it to be the last image she had of him. He intuited correctly; in one of the windowless openings Madera Bree watched him.

Jack Levers was not the only man attempting to force Madera Bree to age. A few days later, two patrons of the Schoolhouse Tap—Tucker and Burt—drove to Madera's house. After they parked Burt's Jeep behind the woods, each of the men reached into the back seat and pulled out a paper bag filled with meat scraps—lamb, beef, chicken, and deer. They hiked up to Madera's house and Tucker unwrapped a package of chicken gizzards, and one by one placed them along the walkway leading to her front door.

"Louise'd whack me hard for spending money on this stuff." He counted his steps out loud. Once he reached five he leaned over, picked up a gizzard between his pinky and thumb finger, and placed it on the ground.

"Shut up! She'll hear us," grumbled Burt.

"Let her hear us. She *knows* we're here. And soon we won't be the only curious creatures."

Burt haphazardly tossed handfuls of cow intestines, livers, and kidneys around the perimeter of the foundation.

"Here, black bears. Here, mountain lions!" called Tucker, meticulously arranging the gizzards.

"There ain't no mountain lions around here," said Burt.

"You never know. This is good grub. They'd like this."

Burt watched Tucker place the scraps on the ground. "You've got to get some in the house. Meat is the thing that'll draw the real wild animals inside."

"Here. You do it." Tucker handed Burt the tray of soupy, veiny parts.

Burt grabbed a fist of guts and let it sail through the windowless opening. "There we go." He prepared to let another missive fly, arm already pulled back, when a flood of water struck him, and then a metal pail lobbed his head. "Fuck!" he yelled. Burt smacked the thighs of his jeans and wrung out the tails of his shirt.

Tucker laughed. "She showed you. That's some old broad, all right."

Burt kicked Madera's door, pounded with his fists. "We'll get you lady! Hear me? I'll come for you myself! When you hear something unfamiliar in the middle of the night, it'll be me."

"Come on," said Tucker. "We'll come back tomorrow, watch all the coyotes and lions scope her property."

"Bastard."

"What'd I do?" asked Tucker. They headed back to the truck, Burt still squeezing water from his clothes and Tucker shaking his head as if there was a pinball inside. "She's something, that's for sure."

"Yeah? Screw you and her both."

*I*t took three hours until she was able to breathe with some regularity. Dusk skirted the trees and still she shook. Madera stepped outside her house uncertainly. She pulled her bad arm in front of her and it wobbled as she walked. Twice she nearly tripped on a rock. She placed a plastic pail on the ground in front of the house and scooped up a few chunks of the animal organs, dropped them in the pail, a slithery wallop. These things hadn't happened when her husband was alive or when she was a child—or had they? Many years ago, if she had spoken, someone would have heard her. Now she kept her thoughts to herself, communicated with the pigs.

When the bucket filled, she dumped it behind the house. Madera took three trips back and forth, dumping the wet feed in the middle of the squealing pigs, thankfully tossing their snouts into the air.

She could not calm her heart. It beat irregularly, as if someone flipped over a cauldron and smacked its bottom like a drum. She tried to get her heart back on track, concentrated on breathing, the methodical whoosh, in and out. It seemed odd that she'd ever breathed without being aware of it.

By the time Jack arrived the following Monday, all signs of Tucker and Burt were gone. He brought another box of mysteries and biographies, three books of poetry and two rolls of gauze. When he held the bandages out she stared at his open fist. "What's this?"

"I just thought you might need some more." She took the bandages from him and held them dumbly in her hand. "Would you let me?" he asked. "Whenever I hurt myself as a kid it always felt better if someone else was able to mend it." Madera rocked the arm against her chest. Slowly, she extended her wounded arm toward him. A faint memory floated out of nowhere: her own mother washing her skinned knees with a bar of lye soap and water, then blowing little puffs of air onto the wound.

Jack's breath caught when the last layer of the cotton T-shirt fell away. "Oh. Jeez." The arm had blackened in places, oozing with puss and a wet sticky film that smelled of overripe tomatoes. She winced. He unwrapped the clean gauze and started covering her arm. "You need to go to the doctor's. I can take you in the van."

She stepped back, holding her injured arm, the gauze falling at her feet. "Leave me alone!" But Jack Levers planned on doing nothing of the sort. He took two giant steps toward Madera Bree and scooped her up. "Put me down!" she yelled as he stepped around the furniture. He carried her toward the van, the pigs crying out, Wee oo oo! Wee oo oo! Wee oo oo! as they made their way through the thin leafed alders and spruce, Jack Levers unwilling to release from his sturdy hands the woman who refused to grow old.

*T*he doctor at Beaver Creek Urgent Care said it was the worst case of first-degree burns he'd ever seen. He prescribed antibiotics for the infection and a white ointment that needed to be applied five times a day. Jack Levers promised the doctor he would make sure she followed each of the instructions, yet Madera didn't murmur a peep. When he let her off at home, he opened the van door and offered to assist her. She batted his hand away, and slid out of the seat. He acted as if he owned her, as if he had some right to do with her as he pleased.

"Bye now!" he sang, waving. She didn't flinch a muscle, fitting her house key in the lock and sharply shutting the door.

The first time he appeared after he'd taken her to the doctor, Madera didn't know what to do. She didn't trust him. She took her willow stick and stood out of sight in the shade of the eaves.

"Ms. Bree? It's Jack Levers. I've brought you more literature."

She tightened her grasp of the stick, tested its point and brushed a whisp of hair out of her eyes. She waited until she heard his footsteps walking away from the house, and then she charged him, her feet kicking up a cloud of dust. She raised the stick and aimed it at the soft spot between his shoulder blades.

He turned toward the noise and the sharp blade of the stick dug in the meat of his shoulder. "Aghhh!"

She regretted it as soon as he fell onto the gravel, pulling the spear from his shoulder and rubbing at the sticky pool of blood. "Are you okay? I'm so sorry. I didn't mean it. It was an accident."

He continued rubbing the torn skin. "We're even now, right? So you can stop being all tough," he said. "We can be friends, right?"

The word hung suspended in the air—*friends*. All hers were deceased. She wasn't even certain she knew what it meant. Did that mean he would make decisions for her? That he would try to rule her life? She wouldn't let him. She offered him her good hand and helped him stand.

The next time he visited, he held out a bag of plums and Madera invited him inside, then immediately regretted it. She left him sitting on the couch while she straightened her books and dusted the corners of the walls. "Looky you!" he persisted, following her from room to room. She didn't know what to say to him, how to act. Madera dipped her head down. "Blue is a lovely color on you. Really lovely."

She straightened her shirt. "It's nothing, this old thing." She waved the idea away with her good hand but couldn't halt the lump that rose in her throat. If he was her friend, was she supposed to share her past with him? Memories made her feel weak. "I can help you with that," said Jack. She stood over the sink, looking outside, absently cradling her arm. Without waiting, he filled the sink with water and slowly submerged her arm.

He lathered his hands with soap and slid them over the bubbled skin. "Does it hurt today?"

Her face curled. The water crept up her arm. "Not much. How about your back?"

"Good as new." Once he finished cleaning and bandaging the wound, Madera opened a drawer and took out a wrapped box. She handed it to him. "What's this for?" he asked.

"For your help."

Jack's lips surfed into a grin. He tore the paper and popped off the lid. He folded back the tissue and found several stacks of twenty-dollar bills.

"I know that's what you want, so here. You've earned it."

"I don't know what you're talking about," said Jack.

"You should. There's good money to be earned if you can get me to gray." Madera held up the ends of her hair. They were as dark as ever.

"I used to want to age you, but now I want to help like any other friend."

"I'm just fine," she said.

"Of course you are." Jack returned the box to its place and shut the drawer.

Madera Bree watched him. She felt herself redden and tingle. Her palms grew sweaty. She smoothed her hair down with her good hand and looked down at her tennis shoes—they were brown and the rubber soles were peeling. She wished she owned a newer pair. As she headed into the backyard, the pigs ran toward her. Wee oo oo! Wee oo oo! Wee oo oo! "I know," she told them, patting the tops of their heads. The pigs ignored Jack and flanked her. She told them, "Check him out. This is Jack." The pigs snorted at him and sniffed his ankles. Madera grabbed a metal bucket filled with pieces of carrots and apples and handed it to Jack.

"What should I do with this?" he asked.

"Feed 'em. They're hungry!"

He chucked handfuls of carrots and apples to the pigs.

"There you go. You've got it." As she watched him move cautiously among her pigs, something swelled inside her.

*J*ack found himself thinking about Madera's long draping hair. He wanted to touch it, let it slide through his fingers; he was growing restless. There were rumors that a group of men were planning to abduct Madera Bree and do things to her. Time was running out.

One evening he developed a taste for the spicy pan-fried

noodles at the Thai restaurant downtown. He described the tangy dish to Madera hoping to pique her interest. Ignoring this suggestion, she instead proposed, "We should play charades! I used to spend every weekend playing this with my girlfriends." She jumped off the couch and positioned herself directly in front of him, already laughing in the way that impressed, gaining fervor like a summer storm.

Even Jack began to chuckle. "How did you ever get to be such a handful?"

She shrugged. But his mind returned to the noodles, and the other restaurants they never visited together.

Sometimes on clear nights Jack and Madera carried folding chairs into the front yard. They drank strong coffee and didn't speak at all. Once Jack gathered the nerve to ask Madera why she still lived in Beaver County.

"A lot of my memories are around here." She pointed with her mug. "I was once married to a good man and this is where we lived." She paused, "Have you ever married?"

He shook his head.

"Well," said Madera. "You'll know her when you're ready."

Jack picked at a mosquito bite with his thumbnail. "I'm interested in someone. She's marvelous. Completely herself."

Madera swallowed. Smoothed her hair. The crickets chirped and Beaver Creek babbled in the distance. "Life is all about chances. You've gotta take 'em," she whispered, forcing her voice to steady.

*J*ack couldn't wait any longer. He was more confused than ever. He arrived at her house early one weekday morning. She answered the door with a toothbrush in her mouth. "Come on," he blurted. "I've got a surprise."

"What? Where?" Madera Bree spit toothpaste into the bushes.

He grabbed the elbow of her good arm and pulled her toward his pickup. She squinted in the sunlight.

"Where are we going?" she asked.

"We're going to do something different. The circus is in Lowell. I want to see the trapeze artists and we can get our faces airbrushed onto matching sweatshirts."

"The circus is for young folks," said Madera Bree. "You go and come back and tell me what you see."

"I won't take no for an answer," he said.

"You're gonna have to." She pivoted and started back. "I'm staying here, where I'm supposed to be."

"Yeah?" He jogged behind her and began tickling her slender waist. He thrust his fingers under her arms. She smelled of a rush of things green and alive—dirt and leaves and twigs. Her skin was more tender and delicate than anything he'd ever touched.

Madera giggled. Her face eclipsed into a wild grin. "Stop! Mercy!"

"Nope!" He seized her and placed her inside the truck. She was still laughing as he locked the door. She quieted. Watched Jack. He slid behind the wheel, his mouth a metal bar.

Her voice faltered. "It's not time. I'm not ready yet." She pointed toward the pigs, "I can't leave them." Jack Levers wouldn't look at her. He started the engine and the truck crept in a slow circle. "Jack, please don't make me do this. I must stay here." He slammed the dashboard with his fist and jerked the car into park.

"Damn it! This is not just about you and what you want."

Madera's fingers fumbled along the side panel, trying to discover how to escape.

"They're going to get you and I'm not going to be able to help at all. I'm not a bad guy. The others will be much worse. You know me. I don't mean you any harm." He opened his door and walked over to the passenger side. She jumped out and the pigs belted out their song. He kicked the tire of the truck with his boot. "You're going to regret this. Do you hear me? Madera?" She didn't answer.

During the evenings Jack Levers continued to visit the Schoolhouse Tavern, and Tucker and Burt would raise their beers as his figure shadowed the doorway. "Grandpa Jack! What are you now, five hundred years old?"

"You guys think you're so smart." Jack took a seat between his friends and ordered a whiskey.

"I hear if you sleep with a woman over a hundred you immediately get fifty more years added onto your life," said Tucker.

Jack rubbed the stubble on his face; it was flecked with white as usual.

"Looks like you're the one getting older," said Burt.

Jack punched Burt's arm.

Sadie lingered in front of them. "Quit that you two. We should be congratulating Jack. Word is there's love in the air—and that's a feat in itself."

"You don't say," said Tucker. "A three-hundred-something-year-old's in love with our Jack Levers."

"It'd boost my ego," added Burt.

"Wouldn't take much."

"Nice one, Sadie," said Burt. "So you two getting married? Honeymoon in the Poconos?"

"Ah, she's a nice old lady," said Jack. "She just isn't very bright. I know what I'm doing."

"We don't doubt you, buddy," said Tucker. "Heck, we've tried. Everyone's tried. Those guys from Lynwood are going to run the old broad out of town for good. What has she ever done for any of us?"

"She's nice to look at," said Jack.

"Well that only goes so far," said Burt.

*E*ven though Madera refused to leave her house, she and Jack continued to see one another. One Saturday, she waited for his arrival. She was eager to tell him about her day, what she thought the pigs were thinking, how much she enjoyed them. Jack had promised to order new windows for her house and when she opened the door to greet him he lugged inside his box of tools. Madera followed behind as he pulled the tape measure across each oblong-shaped window. "My husband—*first* husband put those in," she explained. "The only original window is the one in the kitchen."

"I guess glass used to be rare back then," said Jack.

"And expensive."

"We should be able to find you something. I know a guy who owns a shop." Jack pulled out a wire-bound notebook from his shirt pocket and wrote down measurements.

"The pigs miss you," said Madera.

"Uh-huh."

"Do you like them?" she asked.

He shrugged.

Madera had planned to make up for their argument by pre-paring a picnic. "I packed us a lunch, thought we could take it outside when we're through here." She moved slowly, crossed back and forth in front of him.

"I'm almost done," he said. "I'll meet you outside after I clean up."

"Then I'll go get things ready for lunch."

Jack waited until he heard the pigs' song before he put down his tools. He wandered through the living room, grabbed a book from one of the stacks, examined the cover, and put it back. He used a finger to rub the puddle of black peeking out from beneath the couch. She was lucky they hadn't burned the house to the ground. He opened the door to her bedroom. It was cooler than the rest of the house, sparsely decorated with a single-sized bed and dresser of dark wood. On top of it, a small homemade frame held a photo. The picture itself was old and crimped; fragments of the film had peeled off. The man in the photo looked directly at the camera, his expression patient and calm. Jack felt a burning in his chest, quick and novel. Enough of this, he thought, his chest feeling clogged. Today was the day.

$T$he pigs clamored around the foot of the hill behind Madera's house, toppling over one another. Jack hiked to the place where she had stretched out a blanket sketched with faint lines. Madera opened a container of potato salad, arranged the fried chicken and unwrapped a stack of fudge brownies she'd iced that morning. She handed him a plate and began to fill it with food before serving herself.

He began eating. Madera was about to spoon potato salad into her mouth when Jack tossed his plate down the hill. The pigs shrieked with delight and attacked the lunch. "Jack?" she asked. "What's wrong?"

"I'm tired of you! You don't do anything. You eat the same things, do the same things day after day and never leave this damn place."

Madera let the spoon drop from her fingers. She placed the plate on the blanket and clutched her healing arm. "I didn't know you felt this way."

"That's just the start of it," he said.

"I've always lived here. Where else is there to go? This is home."

"I guess that will always be the difference between us two." Jack looked out across the dense forest. Farther on was downtown Beaver County with its help wanted signs and notices for garage sales; the number of unemployed increased every day. His voice suddenly darkened, grew menacing. "I'm sick of your stupid round house and your ugly stinking pigs. You're supposed to eat them; instead you let them nearly eat you out of all you have." Jack grabbed her shoulders and shook Madera. "Everything about you is so boring. It's as if you died long ago." He took off down the hill, arms swinging wildly. The pigs tossed their heads in the air and brushed their feathery snouts against his pants.

Madera cried. His words rolled through her head, swishing and swirling, making her dizzy. He didn't want to share in her stories. Maybe he was right; her life had already ended. It was okay. She was ready to go. She remained on top of the hill, underneath the fingered canopy of the willow until the sun flashed its nectar and slunk away. The sky bloomed into bruised shades that smeared the horizon, Madera Bree's insides turned outwards, stabbing through the empty spaces of the huddling trees.

Madera Bree did not age. Even Jack Lever's acerbic words could not force wrinkles to groove her face or liver spots to cover her hands. That night she slept outside underneath the flickering landscape of stars. She ripped off her clothes and painted her belly and face, legs and buttocks with the pigs' mud, their pungent feces decorated her supple skin, coating the hollowness of her belly, cupping the space beneath her arms and crinkling the edges of her eyes. She nestled among the pigs with their cool supple skin and felt-tipped ears, their grassy scent finally overlapping with the woman they loved. Madera Bree slept soundly, the languorous dance of dreams spinning in her head.

Two days later Jack returned, planning to find Madera old and wrinkled, looking like a woman of eighty rather than one of eighteen. It was one of the hottest days of the summer and Jack found her in the back of the house, on her knees, her bare buttocks in the air. She was grinding her face into the earth, which had grown dry and dusty. The sun had baked her into an even olive. He yelled at her, "Madera!" and placed a rough hand on her shoulder. "Come on. We'll get you cleaned up." She made a sharp squeal and several pigs swarmed around her. One of them pushed Jack Levers from behind, and he fell onto the ground. "Leave me alone you stupid idiots!" Dirt and scraps of lettuce and carrots stuck to his palms. He slapped his hands together, pushed himself up. He was nearly upright when a sow slammed into him and Jack Levers dove head first into the empty trough, metal clanging. Their squealing pounded against his ears. He covered his face and rolled on his side.

Jack Levers' tears soaked into the dirt, the hot stench of pig slicing through his nostrils. They jostled and bustled around him. "Madera. Please!" Madera Bree was twirling in the dirt, smiling, the dust collecting in her long and matting clumps of hair. Wee oo oo! Wee oo oo! Wee oo oo! Sang the pigs. Jack's sobs grew louder until he was underneath the pigs' heavy bellies. Hidden by their joyous cries, Jack Levers could make any sound necessary. And many became necessary. Madera and the pigs disguised his sharp screams and pleadings. From farther out rose the sound of the low rushing water of Beaver Creek as if it was flowing right beside them—a sound jarring and content—one long, satiated murmur. Saliva glistened on the warming jowls of the pigs as they sang in unison, Wee oo oo!

## Madera Bree

Wee oo oo! Wee oo oo! Madera Bree remained on her knees and led them as they worked, faces turned up to the sun.

# The Longest Pregnancy

$A$nesa Clifford was pregnant for six years. Her pallid eyes blazed behind dark bangs and she slumped beneath the weight of lethargy. She rarely spoke with anyone beside her customers at Fields who begged her for skincare advice. In April of 1986, when she spoke to me, I was fifteen and overweight, certain my life would always consist of oversized sweaters and dumpy blouses.

For the first two years of her pregnancy she worked in the junior department at Fields before they moved her to cosmetics where she would be less visible. They fit her with a gaping white smock and placed her behind the glass counter of Nuero skin and beauty care. Anesa wore her hair pulled into a roll at the back of her neck and her skin gave off a pearly glimmer. At the time, I thought it was the result of dusting herself with Nuero lumines-cent powder. While working at Fields, women were not afraid to stand near Anesa. They offered her the backs of their hands, so she could smooth on the latest age-defying moisturizer, as she raved about the newest lip colors. Behind the counter and dressed in the smock she looked like any other woman in her twenties, attractive in a clearly defined way. During the hours she worked, Anesa could forget her protruding belly, the baby who would not come.

Meanwhile, my brother was also settling into life after returning from a stint in the Army. Only his life was the one he'd left at eighteen. He downed bottles of beer with his high school buddies on the shore of Lake Michigan and also started fixing things—blenders and wristwatches, a grilled sandwich maker—mechanical things he found hidden in our house beneath grocery bags and old phonebooks. I can imagine him at this time in his wood-paneled bedroom at two or three in the morning, lying on the narrow mattress, grease chipped underneath his chewed nails, one arm folded behind his head while he waited for a change.

The first time Pete met Anesa she was on the breakwater overlooking Lake Michigan. Her hair was wet, streaming down her back and her profile was a series of gradual swellings. She was wearing a gauzy dress that clung to her full belly. The sky shone translucent and with it behind her, Anesa looked as if she deserved to perch on the hood of a newly-waxed sports car. Daylight dwindled and crunched-up beer cans surrounded Pete. He still relied on beer, like our father; the morning didn't begin before either had finished a six-pack. He was waiting for his friends to get off work so he could meet them for pitchers at the Whistle Stop. From where Pete sat, he swore he only saw jagged, scissored rocks.

Anesa had stopped waiting for the birth years ago. She no longer watched her calcium and zinc intake and went days without eating a single piece of fruit. She stopped believing it would ever come and told me she had never really wanted it in the first place. She stopped visiting doctors—they weren't much help. The last one she met claimed she was due "in a few weeks" and performed another ultrasound as if the grainy black and white image, the curling tendril of fetus, would somehow make the future birth a reality.

On the shores of Lake Michigan, Anesa cupped the roundness of her belly and looked as if she was trying to pull the mound away from her body and toss it aside, a prosthesis pregnancy. She was touching her stomach the moment Pete watched her step off the rocks and into the tumbling surf. He tossed the can that had grown warm and ran toward her, sand kicking up behind him; he pumped his arms like he was back in training at Fort Bragg. Pulling his knees high over the waves he dove, water exploding into clumsy spray. Pete's arms scrapped the slick sides of rocks and the whitecaps tossed his form, spun him around. He closed his fingers, slapped and dug at keen waves pushing against his face. His chest heaved and his shirt sagged. The rocks snapped at his legs, pointed edges burrowed into his soft spots. Pete made a circle in the water, then burst up, gathered air, aligned himself with the rocky outcrop where the woman last stood and dove again. Water sloshed into his eyes, momentarily concealed his vision. Fatigue moved in. He remained underwater for longer stretches, felt his body tighten and chill. The cadence of waves over his head beat him down, pressed him beneath the surface. His pulse pounded his temples. The surf pushed him farther out.

He felt her hair first. A flimsy ground cover, it webbed his short, wide fingers below the surface, where she waited for the blackness to pervade. Pete loved her at that moment. Before he placed his arms around her back, feeling the heft of her belly beneath his palm. Before he brought her ashore and breathed into her.

Love is not intended for women pregnant six years straight.

Lying in the cold sand, wet dress pushed to her hips, Anesa's skin was chalky. Snot hung from her nose, but Pete left it there, suddenly aware of her blinking eyes focused on him. Her hair was coated in sand and to Pete it looked like she had been rolled in cinnamon. Gulls squawked. She brought one hand to her belly, rolled one side of her face against the sand and began to cry. A pasty cumulus passed overhead. A car sped along the highway. Pete kneaded her limbs and checked for broken bones, the extent of his first-aid training. Anesa felt his warm hands against her legs and shot up, gasping. She opened her mouth and dug her teeth into his shoulder.

"Fuck! What the fuck?" Pete screamed. He stood rubbing his shoulder, watching red dots appear beneath the broken skin. "You're crazy!"

Anesa shuddered, her breathing raked and shallow. Her hands plummeted into the sand on either side of her. She pushed off and stood, wobbling in the uneven heaps of beach.

"You need to stay in one place," said Pete. "I'm going to call for an ambulance." He put his hand out, thought better of it, and gestured at air. "You and your baby need to be checked out." She looked at his shoulder, decorated with a tattoo of a blazing sun. Perhaps she did not speak English. He considered she might be deaf. He slowed down his words. "Let me give you a ride," and mimed the steering of a car.

She shook her head no and limped off to a rusty bicycle reclining in the sand. Anesa tugged at its handlebars, dragged it over to the pavement, and pushed off with her bare feet.

The kids living in Crestview started most of the rumors. They said that a lake monster had crept into Anesa's bed and impregnated her. Some believed that Anesa was a witch and it took many years to birth another witch, the longer its term, the more evil the child would become. The adults were no better. They looked away when they passed Anesa at Sterk's Market or stared at her belly while pretending to read the ingredients on a box of oatmeal. Anesa became used to it, forced herself to focus on the grocery list in her hand. She rarely touched her stomach, neither acknowledged nor denied its existence. Her pregnancy became a kind of mask, much like the makeup she used to accentuate the features of the penny loafer-wearing women at the Nuero counter.

Perhaps she talked to me because I was only fifteen and she pitied my ugliness. My stubby chunkiness was only accentuated by my awkward dress. I wore bright orange and fuchsia—clown colors—purchased in the plus section of Sears, where my father dropped me off with a wad of bills during the first week of August. I didn't know what else to purchase. I bought the first things I saw and vibrant colors always caught my eye. Clothes, like makeup, emphasize and draw attention to certain features. For people like Anesa and me, we had no way of making sure others looked at us for the right reasons. With cosmetics we controlled what they saw.

My nose was too large for my face—it widened at the end as if someone had unsuccessfully tried to flatten it. After school, I spent my time at River Oaks Mall wrapping leopard-print scarves around my neck, trying on wide-brimmed straw hats or velour berets. I saved the makeup counters for last, spritzing my wrist with perfume, sampling lipsticks on the underside of my wrist. "Can I help you find something?" Anesa asked me the first time I met her at Fields. When she smiled all her teeth lined up like white sheets on a clothesline. I thought she was beautiful. I knew who she was. I had heard of Anesa and her pregnancy. I shook my head no, but she still stepped out from behind the Nuero counter and patted the high-backed seat. "Why don't you let me try some products on you? They are all hypo-allergenic." She patted the seat again and I clambered up, feet dangling. She pushed my hair behind my ears and dotted beige cream along my cheekbones. "Are you enjoying your day?" she asked. "Is your mother here with you?"

I told her yes to the first question, no to the second, explaining that my mom passed on when I was a kid. I watched her. I could tell a lot about a person depending on how they reacted to grief.

"Dear. I am so sorry." She placed a thumb on my chin for a moment. Maybe she figured she'd be safe with me, that a motherless child was the perfect confidant. She instructed me, "Always put your makeup on in light that is closest to the environment you'll be working. Stand near the window with a mirror in hand if need be." She asked me a lot of questions, yet offered little information herself. I had the feeling Anesa Clifford was drying up from lack of conversation. "What school do you go to?" she asked. "Do you have a best friend? What are your hobbies?"

Crestview High and no, I told her. I mentioned I liked to read and watch TV game shows. I told her the truth: "I bowled once and the ball rolled backward from my hands."

"I don't care much for sports myself," Anesa confided. "There." She put down a brush and a round pot. She angled the mirror on the glass counter toward me. "You're a pretty girl now, but someday you're going to be quite a looker."

I looked down at my expansive pants baggy through the hips. They pinched me in the middle, left red rings around my stomach. I thanked her quietly. I wanted to believe her and I kept returning, hoping with each visit her prediction might become true.

*P*ete had always been good at putting things together. Before he left for the Army he assembled my Barbie car and fixed the chain on my bike so it didn't slip off each time I pedaled.

After he returned, when he wasn't out with his friends or driving around, he'd stretch out an old sheet in the backyard and adorn it with stray pieces of a lawn mower or some appliance. The mower hadn't worked in years, but Pete figured out how to make it run just by looking at a blade, a slice of plastic, a handful of bolts. He made a little money, and he could drink his beer while working from home. The people in Crestview who had watched Pete mature from a Boy Scout to newspaper carrier and now repairman, began to bring over black and white TVs, food processors, box fans. From my bedroom window I'd watch his sooty fingers fiddle with washers and screws. He could make any machine thrum like it was new.

I suppose in some way he figured he could repair Anesa. The Saturday following her rescue Pete was returning from the Whistle Stop, driving his rusty Monte Carlo. He'd purchased potato chips and a case of Budweiser, the breeze from the open windows splitting his hair into Vs. He was just beyond the beach parking lot, gazing at the expanse of Lake Michigan, when he saw Anesa. She stood on the same rocky plank, this time dressed in a sweater and jeans rolled at the ankles. Pete leaned on the horn and turned the wheel sharply toward the beach. I'd watched him finish three beers with breakfast and four more that afternoon while tooling with a VCR that wouldn't rewind. He held a can of beer open between his thighs. Pete hadn't planned on the shoulder coming so quickly, or the sand being so soft. It happened in slow motion. The back wheels threw up gravel, the car tailed and spun, flipped up on one side and then rolled onto the hood and flipped again, right side up.

Anesa heard the screech of tires, the crash of metal. She touched her belly. Today the water was calm, waves rolled in gentle peaks. She could easily drift off unnoticed. For a minute or two, she hesitated before rushing to the payphone near the vending machines. From shore she watched them lift Pete into the back of the white truck, flashing red and blue lights, the siren a thin wail.

Two days later, Pete stood on the same rocky outcrop, bandaged, waiting for Anesa. He looked gray and thin. Someone at the hospital slipped him Antabuse, he'd claim every day thereafter; one sip of beer made him violently ill, as if all the years he had been drinking revolted against him. Anesa steered her bicycle to the sand and slipped off the seat.

Pete walked over to her, a thin arch of blue thread over his cheekbone. He held out his hand, introduced himself. "It's nice to meet you on land," he said, grinning.

Anesa was not interested in dating. She had lived in Crestview for years and had only carried on conversations with her clients. Pete insisted on driving her home. During the twenty-minute ride, he told her everything about himself—how he'd enlisted in the Army right after high school and hated every moment of his three-year commitment. "People were constantly telling me what to do. Any time I had a free thought someone would reach in and strangle it. I'm good with my hands. I haven't smoked pot in four months and probably won't again." He hesitated. "Unless you want to." Anesa sat in silence, let her body rock with the turning car. When they arrived at her house she thanked Pete for the ride and popped open the door. Pete lugged her bike from the trunk, its tires pinging on the sidewalk. "Can I come in?" he asked.

Anesa grabbed hold of the handlebars. "I don't think that would be a good idea."

He leaned in toward her lips and Anesa ducked, pretended to wipe something off her shoe. She turned to him, looked at her belly. "I've been pregnant for six years."

Pete grinned, and the sides of his face widened. "Quality takes a bit longer," he said, taking one of her hands and squeezing it.

$P$ete visited River Oaks Mall wearing a baseball cap slung low over his eyes. He lurked behind the handkerchiefs and wallets, the perfect straightaway to Anesa's counter. He watched her lift bottles with the ends of her fingers, cradle compacts, and display them to clients with a gentle sway of her wrist. She touched women's faces with serene ease, glided over wrinkles with triangular sponges, penciled in nonexistent brows, and used a tiny brush to smooth powder onto eyelids. But I was the one she invited over to her apartment the second time I hipped up to the Nuero counter. "It's nice to see you," she told me. "Did you have a good day at school? Did you learn anything useful?"

I smiled at her shyly, lifted a fragrance to my nose. "That's for summer," she said. "It's called Bath. What do you think of that name?"

I shrugged.

"It's too fruity for that name," she said.

I sniffed it again.

"I would have chosen Bounty or Rendezvous—something that goes along with summer vacations. Bath? It doesn't make me think of anything." She looked at her watch. "Can I give you a ride home? Or better yet, you should come over. I have some makeup samples you can have." I hadn't been invited over to someone's house since the second grade when my mom was healthy and made Rice Krispie treats for me to give my friends.

Anesa's car was long and cream-colored. My chin just tipped over the dashboard. I leaned my head back and watched the houses blur past as it rained dull lazy drops. She turned on soft music, the kind older couples swayed to.

At her house we sat on a green couch with two crocheted

pillows, sipping tea from mugs that looked new, not chipped and stained like ours at home. Posters of the four seasons of nature hung from the walls. Autumn was a close-up of an oak with red and gold leaves; two leaves were in the process of dropping to the ground. Spring was a grassy meadow with three butterflies sorting through the skies. Anesa put a hand on her belly. "I'm sure you're curious so we'll just stop the questions right here. Do you know how babies are made?"

I nodded.

"This one got here that way, too, only it was a bit different. It happened one August afternoon when I was still living with my daddy in Indiana. At home I worked as a makeup artist for an undertaker and at night I used to take walks along West Beach to clear my mind." Anesa took a deep breath and looked at her knees. "One evening when I was out walking, the sky turned black and hard gusts started blowing fast. This was followed by thunderclaps, a shower of sparks. I woke on my stomach in a pool of blood."

"Were you struck by lightning?"

Anesa nodded, started fingering the hem of her skirt. "I couldn't stick around my hometown after the accident. People talked when I started showing. My daddy still had a life to live. I couldn't ruin that for him. So now you know the truth. And you can tell whoever you want. It's no secret."

Even I knew when I was being told an untruth. However, I decided I would be honest with her. "Sometimes kids at school call me names."

"Names?" she asked. "Like what?"

"The last few weeks it's been Attila the Hun. This week, Buster Bar, like the ice cream treat."

"Well, at least it's something good to eat," said Anesa. "They used to call me Flubbo. I still don't know what a Flubbo is."

I must have looked surprised.

"I used to weigh 176 pounds." She patted my knee. "You'll slim down. Don't worry. Sometimes the body works in weird ways."

*A*nesa finally invited Pete inside her house but only for short visits. He found broken things and fixed them. A toaster and a floor lamp with a fat chunk of pine as a base, a ceramic humming-bird that spun on a dish singing, "You Light Up My Life." She took the fixed items in her hands. "Thank you for all your kindness," she said, and then after Pete left, returned the objects to her basement. Anesa was surprised to find him at her door when she returned from work one evening. She hadn't invited him, yet there he stood on her porch beside a renovated vanity. He carted the vanity into the kitchen and she walked around it, sat on the white chrome stool, flicked on the tray of bulbs surrounding the mirror.

"It's yours now. I want you to have this," he said. Pete sat at the kitchen table on a fold-up chair, staring at her, the tea pot just beginning to sputter.

"I don't need it, Pete. I have no use for things that I don't need." Anesa stood up and took out two cups and saucers, opened a box of vanilla wafers and arranged them in a circle on a plate.

"How do you know you don't need it unless you try it out?"

"I just know," said Anesa. "It just isn't right. Like us, we aren't right," said Anesa.

"What could possibly be wrong with us?" Pete asked.

"It's not you, it's me. You deserve more than me." Her forehead crimped and furrowed.

Pete made a fist and the sun on his biceps thinned and expanded. "You don't know what I deserve. 'Cause if you did, you'd say I wasn't good enough for you."

"You don't want a woman like me," she said. "I've done bad things. Things that aren't right." Anesa grazed her stomach.

"Why don't you just say you aren't attracted to me?"

Anesa was quiet. A tangerine hue from the streetlights glimmered through the window. "I'm not looking to get involved," she said.

Pete continued, "Just give me time. A few weeks. Give yourself the chance to know me. If you still hate my guts I'll leave you alone." Pete held up a hand. "Scout's honor."

*A*nesa tried to become an optimist. She changed her hours at Fields so she would be available evenings. Meanwhile, Pete started working for Mr. Kopilash, who owned a small repair shop downtown.

Every Tuesday and Thursday night, he drove to her house. Some nights they attended fish fries at the VFW and afterward worked on a jigsaw puzzle of a family of primates. In the process, Pete screeched like an ape and scratched his armpits until Anesa covered her mouth, unable to halt the laughter spilling over her fingers. They rode bikes along the path in the forest preserve, Anesa pointing out the leaves of paper birches, larkspur, and sugar maples already tinged with color. Pete talked about their future. "We don't always have to live in Crestview. The schools aren't the best."

Anesa averted her eyes or licked her lips.

He asked, "Is there somewhere you'd like to live?"

She pretended not to hear him.

Anesa was surprised when she discovered Pete was my brother. He had brought her back to our house to meet our dad after one of their dates. Anesa seemed quieter than when I visited her counter at Fields, but she gave me a quick, fierce hug when we were introduced, and whispered in my ear to come by the counter soon. She must have told Pete how we knew each other because later that night when he returned, he came into my room and sat on my bed. Pete seldom had time for me and here he was, seeking me out. I was reading a horror novel and glad to see him. "Anesa really likes you," he said. I'm certain I beamed. He squeezed the blanket where my leg was hiding. "'Night, kiddo."

They both took Wednesday afternoons off. Pete insisted on giving Anesa swim lessons. "I don't ever want to find you in water unless you're floating or bathing," he said, while shaking his finger at her. She wore a pink suit that scooped at her neck and fell into a ruffled skirt. It was made for an overweight woman and Anesa's stomach pushed the skirt up, splicing her mid-belly. Pete held Anesa's hand as they approached the water.

"Let go," she said. "I'm all right." Anesa stood and stared at the water for some minutes, while Pete strode knee-deep into the surf, water dripping down the hairs on his legs. "Okay," she announced.

Pete walked closer to shore where she stood, took her hand and they entered the lake together. He taught her how to breathe in the water, forcing the air out in bubbles. They practiced floating on their stomachs, then backs. Pete walked out until the water hit him waist deep and demonstrated the flutter kick. "Now you try."

Anesa straightened the straps on her suit, put her arms in front of her and kicked.

"You've got it!" Pete exuded the same victorious tone when he heard an engine erupting out of silence.

Anesa grinned broadly. "I want to do it again."

"Who am I to stop you?" Pete motioned his arm at the lake. "It's all yours."

Face down, Anesa held her arms overhead and kicked. "That's my girl," said Pete. With her face in the water, stomach down, the hum of the surf in her ears, Anesa floated.

He cradled her. She leaned her head back and rested her cheek against his shoulder. He carried her out of the water like this, as if he was carrying her across the wedding threshold, and placed her on a bedspread they'd stretched behind a cove of trees. Pete sat beside Anesa and used a towel to dry each of her arms and legs, each hand and foot. His fingertips brushed the pink straps. He drew the blanket around their shoulders. Her hands and toes were icy, but her face flushed warm. He undressed them both and pressed himself against her, his body melding around the heft of her belly. They nested into each other, rolled together while the moon whitened and the day reddened, then dropped.

*T*he day following a twelve-hour sale at Fields, when the store was unnaturally quiet, Anesa invited me over. She brought a case of makeup home with her and arranged two chairs near the largest windows. She brushed my hair behind my ears and started smoothing foundation onto my skin, then suddenly asked me if I missed my mom.

I told her I only remembered scraps and fragments, her body stretched out on the living room couch, the radio always blaring country songs.

Anesa nodded. "My mom left me, too. Only she wasn't sick. She was just tired of us."

"What happened?" I asked.

Anesa flicked her fingers. "You know, just one of those things. We did something wrong, I guess. Have you ever felt intense pain?"

I told her I had not.

"After you're struck by lightning it's hard to make sense of anything. Your body is no longer your own—it cramps up and you ache. I was in bed for weeks after the accident."

I admitted a similar outlook: "I feel that way too, sometimes. Like I have no power over my weight."

"You're a lovely girl," said Anesa.

"Thanks." While she smoothed makeup onto my face and told me about her recovery from the lightning, I imagined the baby's father. He had probably been watching her for days before he pounced, dragging her into an alley and taking advantage of her, his dirty stubble scraping her skin. "I'm sorry," I blurted.

"For what?"

"For everything," I said.

"I met you, didn't I? Things are good." Anesa pulled three lipsticks out of her bag. "Which one do you like better?" I picked out a shade called raspberry truffle.

"Yes. A good choice for you." She asked me if I had a boyfriend.

I shook my head no.

"That's okay. You don't want a teenage boy. Bad for your complexion." She picked the mirror up and handed it to me. "You have to be careful with men. You can't trust them no matter what they say."

I wondered if she thought the same thing about my brother.

*P*ete made plans for the eventual birth. He bought diapers and towels in the shape of ducks, a yellow plastic bathtub and terrycloth sleepers. In our attic, he found the crib we had each used as infants. He stripped the varnish, added a coat of paint, and hid it in the garage. Pete opened a savings account and accepted more work from Mr. Kopilash. He woke up with me in the morning, fixed us both a hard-boiled egg or cereal. He started picking me up from school and afterward seemed pleased to drop me off at the mall.

Once when Anesa stood over me at Fields, giving me evening eyes, she said, "These are the eyes you'll wear out on the town when your boyfriend takes you out to show you off."

I felt her hard belly against my knee and suddenly wanted to ask her about her pregnancy. "Does it hurt to be pregnant?"

She held the applicator midair. "No. It doesn't hurt." Anesa thought for a minute, her face screwing up in bits. She put down the eye shadow and swiveled the chair so I faced her fully. Her eyes grew pointy. "What do they say about me now?" Her voice escalated. "What have you heard? Are they still saying I'm Godzilla's bride? That I'm being punished for some crime? That it's a tumor, or I'm riddled with cancer?" She bent over me and I could smell the mintiness of her breath.

"Are you?" I asked.

"Huh?" She was crying a bit. "Oh, dear. I'm sorry." She dabbed at her eyes with a Kleenex and peered into the mirror. "Come home with me tonight. I'll make tuna." She patted my fat thigh. "Don't you believe a thing anybody tells you. You just take your time, okay?" I promised her I would. "That's good. Now these eyes, let's see." And she took the ball of her pinky and closed each one of my eyelids.

*I* slumped on the couch while she fixed our dinner. She opened a TV tray in front of the two of us so we both had somewhere to place our mugs of instant coffee. She went into the kitchen and brought back two heaping plates of tuna casserole. She placed a paper napkin near my hand. "Let me know if you need anything."

I told her it tasted good. "Well, you probably don't eat many homemade meals like this," she said. She started with her questions again. "Have you started to think what you might like to do in the future?"

I shook my head.

"Every girl needs a plan. Will you remember that?" I promised I would, filled a forkful with casserole, and stuffed it in my mouth.

"What are your plans?" I asked. "Are you going to marry Pete?"

"Wow." She looked shocked. "Did he tell you to ask me that?"

I shook my head. "I was just curious."

Anesa put down her fork and wiped her mouth with a napkin. "No one sees the future. Who knows what will be? If you can, you want to allow yourself as many choices as possible. Like when I make up your face. I'd rather use less product and add on to that first layer than use too much and have to take it all off."

"Does Pete know you were struck by lightning?"

"What? Sure he does."

"Do you think you'll ever have the baby?"

Anesa took a sip of coffee and pressed her finger against a crumb that'd fallen on her sweater. She rubbed two fingers together and dropped the bit onto her plate. "I doubt it."

*P*ete and Anesa went to the movies or dined on burgers at Miner Dunn's. If they were going to be in a public place, Anesa disguised herself behind a trench coat. On one of the hottest days of the year, the carnival came to town. "It's nearly one hundred percent humidity out here," said Pete. His hand was on the back of her long coat as he led her toward his car. "You're going to boil."

"So I'll boil."

"You're beautiful the way you are."

"Pete, please don't start this now. When we first met I was pregnant and I'm still pregnant I—"

Pete lifted a hand and swatted at the air as if he could get rid of the entire topic.

When they arrived at the carnival they walked beneath a banner of balloons. Clowns pushed carts of cotton candy and candied apples, while a man with a five-gallon high hat balanced on a unicycle. Anesa wanted to ride the Zebulon with its quadruple dip and upside down loops even though the posted sign warned against riders who suffered from heart disease or other physical ailments. "Come on, I'll be fine." She pulled Pete's hand toward the snaking line.

Pete broke her grasp and walked over to a giant bumblebee that was painted yellow and black. He watched it spin toddlers on the seats curled inside the bee. She joined him, her mouth flipped downwards. It was an old argument. He turned to her and said, "It's partly you. I love the baby. I love you." Pete placed his hand on Anesa's middle. "I don't care who he was. How you met him."

Anesa's eyes whipped up at his face, her mouth a fine line. "I think we should leave." She began walking and used a hand to keep the flaps of her trench coat closed. She headed toward the grassy field where they had parked. There were puddles of mud left over from the afternoon's storm, but Anesa stomped right through them, unaware of the muddy drops splattering her coat.

Pete called out to her from behind, swung his arms and jogged to catch up. "I want you to live with me. I want to wake up next to you for the rest of my life."

"I'm sorry, Pete." She shook her head, wouldn't turn around, her hand on the car door. "I can't. Please take me home."

$F$or two weeks straight he came to the counter at Fields and pleaded his case. Anesa ignored him, sprayed the glass with cleaner and wiped it with a paper towel. Pete swore. "Damn it! Anesa, listen to me!" Management moved her to gift wrap in the back of the store until things between the two calmed down.

I didn't talk to her while she was working gift wrap, too many nosy grandmother-types wrapping boxes alongside her. While she was ignoring Pete, I felt as if she was breaking up with me as well. I doubled the size of my lunches and hid jumbo-sized bags of corn chips in my book bag. I cleared the makeup from the top of my dresser and hid it in a shoebox. When Anesa returned to the Nuero counter, she seemed generally less interested in talking. She fiddled with the arrangement of containers on the shelves and took to checking her wristwatch. I was thrilled to see her and waited for her to invite me over, and makeup my face. It took several minutes before she even realized I was there.

"Hello," said Anesa feebly. She offered me a ride home but she didn't invite me inside her house and, gradually, I began to spend afternoons in my bedroom again.

Pete left flowers on Anesa's step. Sometimes he sat on the curb, waited for her to return after her shift. When she saw him there, Anesa would turn around in the nearest driveway and aimlessly drive along the streets of Crestview until he left.

Every afternoon Pete drove to the beach and watched Anesa swim up and down the shore, her elbows peaked high, her hands making perfect, splashless entries. She wore a white cap and sometimes Pete could see the ends of her brown hair peeking out. He bent over the rocks and watched over her, counted her strokes. Sometimes he'd hide until he saw her stepping into the water, or he waited in the dark, watched her diamond-shaped figure pedal off on her bike, and then he stretched out in the sand, the waves talking to him in small, clipped phrases.

When the pains came, Anesa was in the basement doing laundry, pulling blouses out of the dryer and placing them on hangers. She was going on her seventh year of pregnancy. Surrounded by balls of lint and stacks of old newspapers, the bulb at the foot of the stairs dim, the sensation must have shocked her.

Meanwhile, Pete was fiddling with a go-cart for a neighborhood boy. Fluorescent light leaked from the garage. Crickets chirped. He was having difficulty getting the steering mechanism to stick. He figured Anesa would ultimately come around if she just had a chunk of time to herself. Pete worked a bit longer on the go-cart, and when his stomach grumbled, he decided to buy himself a hamburger. It was after nine, and as he started the car an autumn wind kicked up sharp, prickly blasts.

By habit, Pete drove by Anesa's house. The rooms were dark. He'd told himself he wouldn't bother her and he'd just leave her be; still, the Monte Carlo instinctively veered toward the curb. He knocked on the door of her house. When she didn't answer, Pete pounded. "Anesa, come on. Let's go for a ride." Pete continued knocking. He circled the house, pounded on each window. No answer. He yelled her name. "Anesa. Answer me!"

Near the back of the house he found a slit in the curtains; this is where he spied Anesa's shape. She was on the floor and she was still. His blood spiked. He took off his boot and swung the heel against the window in the kitchen—glass shattered. He cleared the jagged pieces from the frame and pushed his upper body through the open space, the faucet stabbing his knee. Anesa's legs were splayed open, surrounded by a puddle. She waved at him with a faint hand.

"Holy shit!" Pete scooped an arm around her back and helped her stand, heaving her weight against him. She mouthed words but no sound followed. "Hospital. Hospital," said Pete.

Because they weren't married nor was Pete part of Anesa's family, the doctors at St. Margaret's wouldn't let him in the room during delivery. He called me, and then went to the gift shop and bought a nightgown for Anesa, a stuffed giraffe, and a small bag of peanut M&Ms. I pilfered some bills from our dad's wallet and took a cab to the hospital. I sat with Pete in the hospital lobby eating his candy, glaring at a TV news show. Pete told me his plans: he'd move into Anesa's place (she had more room) and once the baby was two years old or so, they would find a house of their own. Mr. Kopilash would hire him full-time and Anesa could become a floater at Fields, working a few times a month during special sales. First, they would have a small ceremony at the house, a reception with sandwiches and cake. He had it all planned.

By the time they allowed Pete to enter the delivery room they had already wrapped the baby in a towel and placed her on Anesa's chest. Pete found them in this position, the baby squirming toward Anesa's neck while she looked off, blankly.

Pete named the baby Amy.

Mr. Kopilash agreed to let him complete repairs from Anesa's garage, so when Amy cried, it was Pete who washed his hands and rushed inside to pick her up. Meanwhile, Anesa remained in bed or she drove to Fields where even though she was on maternity leave, she'd stand in front of the Nuero counter fingering eye shadows or straightening bottles of lotion and pore clarifier.

Pete seemed more centered than ever. He was confident once Anesa saw how beautiful Amy was she'd be content and share in the joy that nearly exploded from his skin. When he came in from the garage at night and she and Amy were both asleep, he picked up the baby and nestled her beneath Anesa's chin. Her eyes sprung open. "Please," Anesa pleaded, her voice splitting.

"Just—"

Anesa shook her head, no, and within moments of taking Amy back into his arms, Anesa rolled on her side, coiled away.

The day she left, Pete was in the garage working on a snow blower. He heard the car door and figured she was going to Fields. He picked up the two parts he was greasing and repositioned himself outside the back door so he could hear Amy when she woke.

The water must have felt cold at first, gradually warming, her stroke returning, the sun on her back, her bra and underwear dragging, filling with water. At some point she must have thrown them off, kept swimming. How many strokes did it take to get to the other side? Now it was Anesa, cutting the waves, making them croon. The water was no longer icy. And perhaps Anesa wondered why she hadn't come here sooner to swim, to let the water carry her until she traveled far enough.

*T*hey found her naked on the shore two towns over. She didn't recall her name, but even without her pregnant belly, the rescuers knew Anesa.

Pete remained certain that with his care and attention, she would get well and things would fall into place. He took turns caring for both Anesa and Amy. Anesa refused to talk. Her eyes glazed over. She didn't seem to recognize anyone. I brought over my small makeup collection to her house, samples she had given me and discounted stuff I purchased at the drugstore. I sat on the side of her bed, the mattress dipping to the wiry springs, and arranged a lamp near her face. I opened the shades and let the sun in. Smoothing her hair back, I dotted her face with concealer, used powder and blusher to warm her cheeks. She looked as beautiful as ever.

One afternoon after I had finished making up her face, Pete and Amy entered the room without knocking. Pete held Amy and strode confidently toward the bed. "It's your mama! Isn't she lovely?" He leaned over and touched Anesa's forehead. While he straightened the blankets around her, Amy lifted her chubby arm, unclasped a fist and waved at her mother. Anesa saw something altogether different that neither Pete nor I witnessed—she saw a flash of light blaze in her daughter's palm. The corners of Anesa's mouth turned up and Pete noticed the change in her expression. "Looky that!" He leaned over and kissed her chin, then gave Amy a slobbery kiss. "You're doing great," he said to Anesa. "You'll be up and about in no time."

"We should let Anesa rest," I said. "She's going to need her energy." As if seeing myself for the first time, the feel of my nose blossoming on my face, the rolls of fat bunching at my thighs. Someday I was going to be slender and beautiful, maybe when I was older. First, I had to believe anything was possible, and that day was miles off.

# The Hunted

$F$ather Tiko had been sitting cross-legged on a fold-up chair watching the Ramblers practice on a makeshift court in the parish basement when Marcy O'Connor's wayward serve sent the volleyball into the heel of his scuffed wingtip. Game attendance was another way the recently-appointed pastor of St. Ann's planned to make himself a fundamental part of the parish. Father Tiko bolted upright, held the ball between his small hands and tossed it to Marcy. He wore eighteen-dollar cotton broadcloth boxers and brushed with whitening toothpaste. His vows pressed against his leg, and yet it was Marcy O'Connor's swishing ponytail galloping back to the court like some decorated pony that caused Father Tiko to pause. Just weeks beyond his fortieth birthday, he remained dazzled.

Two weeks later, Marcy sat curled in the passenger seat of Father Tiko's Impala. The heat was on full blast and he was certain his shoes were melting. Marcy had a cold, so she breathed out of her mouth, a gentle whirring, like a ceiling fan. He was driving them to Hunted Trails, a local wildlife park stocked with free-roaming animals of varying species. And while he didn't normally support such amusements, it was a private location within driving distance.

"Should be the next light. You'll take a right." Marcy held the rumpled directions between her red mittens. Father Tiko didn't plan on enjoying Hunted Trails, although Marcy spoke fondly of it each time he mentioned he enjoyed her company. Clearly, they wanted to get to know each other better.

She had visited Hunted Trails as a child and was chased by an ostrich when she snuck away from her parents. This had not surprised him for Marcy seemed like she had been a precocious child.

"This it?"

"You got it, Father T."

Sheets of snow concealed the unplowed road. Branches were dressed in powdery white veils and intricate lace-like patterns dusted bushes. They turned east and the tires of the Impala slipped, squealing on the layers of frozen and refrozen snow. As they neared Hunted Trails, the road narrowed, a peaked incline. He craned his neck from side to side until it popped. "That's gross," said Marcy and Father Tiko laughed quickly, as if Marcy had told him he was one of her very good friends.

Father Tiko wasn't concerned about supposed animals trained to chase humans at Hunted Trails. Or the steep hills. He used the treadmill in the basement in the rectory four times a week and although his scalp had begun to show through his black hair, he felt strong and youthful. In fact in the fifteen days since the volleyball spun into his foot, Father Tiko had begun to feel altogether perfect, and he had Marcy's mossy eyes to thank. After the incident in the gymnasium, Father Tiko discovered (and jotted down in his loopy scrawl) the following:

*Marcy lived with her parents in Knollwood Estates;*

*Her father painted houses;*
*Her mother worked as a florist out of their basement;*
*Marcy's PSAT scores: 870;*
*She wore contacts and suffered from seasonal allergies;*
*She received one detention last year for kissing a basketball player from*
Mt. Carmel after the semifinals.

Marcy sniffed and wiped her nose on her sleeve. She sounded like a clogged drain. "God, I wish I felt better."

"Well . . . I'm sure he's trying." Really, HE was the last person Father Tiko wanted to consider. He had told some falsehoods to steal Marcy away from her classes even appointing her to the Priest's Council, a new advisory board that consisted of one memeber. Father Tiko wore dark baggy jeans, like the students in his youth group, and a gray sweater that Marcy had mentioned was a nice color on him. They passed a large midsection of a tree crookedly rolled onto its side. It welcomed them to Hunted Trails in red fat dripping letters that looked as if they had just been painted.

"Awesome!" said Marcy.

The trees drooped under the white weight. Tiny leafless shrubs and snowdrifts waved on both sides of the street. They stopped the car at a gate beside a wood hut. Father Tiko rolled down the window. A man in an olive jumpsuit, purple beret, and clipboard stepped out. "Howdy, folks." His breath escaped in slow clouds that hung over the car door like two expectant balloons. The sky glinted, a pearly blue marble. He handed over two consent forms. "Student discount if you have ID," he knocked on the board in his hands.

"Let me see." Marcy dug through her wallet. A giant metal butterfly dangled from the coin zipper. She fumbled with various scraps of paper. Father Tiko figured it was the same type of wallet a fifth-grader might own and he momentarily felt annoyed with himself for realizing it. Marcy reached an arm across him to hand the guard her ID, and the scent of her floral shampoo speared his nostrils. A ball churned warm in his belly. He pulled out a fifty-dollar bill from his wallet and handed over their signed consents.

The guard tucked his head into the open window. "Been here before?"

Father Tiko shook his head no, and Marcy sniffled a yeah.

The guard clipped their forms to his board. "Well, you're both in for a treat. Just got two Bengal tigers this fall. I just need to ask you some questions and you'll be on your way." He straightened his shoulders. "Do you understand you are responsible for your own safety?"

"Yes," they chimed.

He checked one of the forms in his hands. "Do you understand that emergency services only provide assistance after one of you has been injured?"

Father Tiko chuckled. The guard stopped and stared, and the eggplant-colored beret made his head appear swollen. "Sure. Of course." His stomach grumbled and Father Tiko patted the mound of his belly. One of the cooks had packed a lunch of fried chicken and fruit breads, and Father Tiko couldn't wait to dig in.

Marcy spoke up. "If you're not ready for this, Father, there's a beginner's park. That's where I went last time. We could do that. They have animals in cages or on leashes so you don't really have to run much."

"Don't be crazy," he said. "We're all about being hunted."

The man smacked a bright sticker on the inside of the windshield. "Enjoy. Be safe."

Father Tiko waved him off and rolled up the window. Marcy unfolded the map and called off directions while alternating glances out the window. "It's so much smaller than I remember it."

He wanted to explain to her that she was a child during her last visit and now, nearly an adult, her perspective had changed. He smiled to himself. She tried to appear mature around him and he wasn't about to dampen her spirit.

"Keep following the main road until you come to a fork," she instructed, "then veer left and follow the signs to the parking area."

He knew if he said anything critical Marcy would see him as an adult, and that was not what he wanted.

"Okey doke." He was still uncertain of his own intentions. If everything in his life was the will of God, did this include his interest in Marcy O'Connor? Perhaps appreciation would better describe his feelings, which brewed warm at the pit of his stomach. The past few days, these same feelings had thrust him out of bed bleary-eyed at three or four in the morning the past few days as he thought about Marcy snug in her twin bed across town, dressed in flannel pajamas with pictures of rainbows dancing across her burgeoning breasts. He considered her breasts again. They were going to be beautiful.

He enjoyed seeing himself in this girl's eyes. Last week she'd asked him if he could change anything in the Catholic Church, what he would alter. He couldn't come up with a thing, so he murmured something about female priests, which Marcy wanted to hear—most of the girls her age held far-reaching criticisms about the gender issue in the Church. He could only imagine. And she had nodded agreeably.

"There's a sign for parking." Marcy pointed with her mitten and it took on the shape of a Labrador's nose. He followed her directions and steered into a space. It was Tuesday and his car was the only one in the lot. While she was supposed to be in class, he was supposed to be administering the sacraments at St. Margaret's Hospital. Luckily, he'd called a deacon from Our Lady of Mercy to take his place. Marcy popped open her door before he even turned off the ignition. "We're really here!"

He slipped out, stretched his arms over his head. "Yep. Hungry?" Father Tiko opened the trunk and pulled out a wicker basket. Marcy came up beside him and sniffed at the food.

"I can't smell a thing," she said.

"That doesn't matter as much as taste."

"Aren't they the same?" asked Marcy.

"We'll have to see about that." Father Tiko grabbed a blanket and headed past the snow-covered picnic benches. The new sneakers he wore rubbed his heel. He'd accept it as penance for fibbing to Marcy's parents. He had told them it was customary for all the Priest Council members to go away for a day of reflection at the parish retreat center. Marcy was a good student and he wasn't concerned that she would forego the assignments missed in class that day, or fail to bend the truth to her parents when they asked about the retreat. He simply wanted to spend more time near her and she seemed to want to learn more about him.

Marcy followed a few feet behind him. "The food might attract bears. Last time I was here there were black bears that followed us."

"Yeah? Black bears are cute," he said. "We'll give them some banana bread."

"I can tell you've never been chased by a wild animal. Once I saw a special about the Waddells. They opened Hunted Trails in the 1970s as an adventure park for thrill-seekers. Mr. Waddell was an ex-zookeeper and the first animals housed in the park were toss-offs that he got for free—aged bears and monkeys or overly violent animals that were going to be put to sleep. Anyhow, since it opened, there have been thirty deaths, including Mr. Waddell, the father of the whole clan."

"Probably some publicity stunt."

"No, it was for real. He kicked a sleeping grizzly after finishing two bottles of whiskey with his buddies from the American Legion. Heck, even *I* know bears aren't true hibernators."

Father Tiko bent over and used the arm of his jacket to clear snow from a patch of ground. Short stubs of frosted grass peeked out and the shot of bland green made Father Tiko think about the all-inclusive power of God. With the low numbers listening to callings and even fewer ordained, Father Tiko was certain that God would save one of his own from being eaten by a large animal at an adventure park.

"One of my cousins worked a summer in the beginner's park and he said that here in the main park they try and make the animals mean so they'll chase you as soon as you're spotted."

He handed the basket to Marcy and spread out a wool blanket checked with black and white squares. Father Tiko kneeled on the blanket and began taking out Tupperware containers. "Well, then we better eat before they eat us!" Father Tiko was certain Hunted Trails was just another version of distraction for people to take their minds off inherent evil, a means of punishing themselves for their commercial ways. What people needed was a recommitment to faith. Most of his parishioners believed only in what they could see, not the unseen. That was another program he hoped to implement at St. Ann's in the next year or so—a support group for the material-obsessed.

Father Tiko believed in the order and sensibility of the Church. Every mass had a specific goal. During the Eucharist he said the same words the disciples uttered thousands of years before him. That connection to a world outside of their town, beyond most of the dull-eyed parishioners of St. Ann's, satisfied him greatly. And now there was Marcy O'Connor to fit into the equation. He had nearly decided she would become another facet of his life, not one of the expectations the Vatican or parishioners held for him, but a means for him to feel more like the man he once was.

Marcy's two front teeth dug into a slice of bread, gummy pastiness filling up the enamel spaces between the silver braces of her orthodonture. Marcy was a loved girl, loved by her parents and friends, no doubt. Father Tiko could feel it all around her— an aura of warmth that he envied. He knew his role in the Church was more vital than ever, and yet it seemed the perfect time to challenge the choice he'd made. If he was a servant of God, shouldn't God also provide him with continual signs that HE was pleased with him? Marcy O'Connor was simply another symbol, like the crucifix or Easter lilies or the purple and pink candles of Advent. Father Tiko believed in all of these traditions. But he was more than just another man of the collar.

He watched Marcy wipe her fingers on her jacket. "Mmm. These are good." She popped another deviled egg into her mouth.

"Do you like eggs, Marcy?"

"Only this way. My mom always soft boils eggs. Yuck—I hate runny yolks."

Father Tiko opened a map of Hunted Trails and smoothed it flat. "Where do you think we should start?" Marcy leaned in next to him and their shoulders touched. A warm wave rolled inside him. He figured they'd walk around a bit then return to the car and stop for a cup of cocoa on the way back.

"I'm open," she said.

"How about terrain three. There are animals from Africa and it says the trails are rigorous," said Father.

"Are you sure you're up for that?" asked Marcy.

"Me? I'm more concerned for you."

"Come on Father, you're talking to a Lady Rambler here."

"Oh, right."

They bundled up the leftovers and placed them in the trunk. Father Tiko bent down and tightened the laces of his new sneakers. He stood and they began walking, feet shuttling dirt and small splotches of snow, bunches of leaves and twigs. The dirt path traversed a sight incline. Marcy took the lead and he adjusted to a smaller step, careful not to lose his balance.

She asked him, "Are you afraid of meeting some animals today, Father?" As they walked on, large rocks dotted the trail amidst fair elders and birches, naked and flimsy.

"There is nothing to fear when God is on your side. You and I both walk in safety because God will save us." The rocks gradually became boulders, ferocious, jagged edges towering up on both sides of them. The stones overtook the path and both Marcy and Father Tiko put their hands up on either side to guide them. Father Tiko slipped sideways between the narrow sections; yellow powder coated his hands. Since Marcy was in front of him, he rubbed the dust on the seat of his jeans.

As they walked, the trees jutted higher. The rocks pushed in farther until they blocked the path altogether. They followed the tiny blue Xs that marked the tree trunks. Marcy cupped her hands on a boulder's two uneven spaces and pulled herself up. She grunted and sniffled, but her foot held firmly until she finally reached the top. She slapped her hands together and stood several feet above Father Tiko, waving at him. "Come on up!"

He tried to recall the places she'd positioned her feet and hands, but he faltered and slipped, tearing a hole in his jeans. Marcy grabbed the back of his jacket and heaved him up. She turned on her heels and marched ahead. Father Tiko took a few steps, but his breath continued to fall fast upon his chest. He stopped and

pulled off his stocking cap, wiping the perspiration from his forehead. "It's beautiful out here," he yelled.

She was already several feet ahead, and turned around, called
out, "Wha?" Then walked back until she stood beside him, huffing
lightly. "There's no one else here." And as Marcy said it, she reached
for Father Tiko's gloved hand and pulled him toward her until
their faces were cloaked in the same filmy breath. "Father. I have
a confession."

Father Tiko's heart blazed in his throat. Dry lips. He licked
his lips. Dry mouth. He hadn't planned on everything taking place
so quickly. He was a man. Just a man.

Marcy blurted: "I made love to Candace Borsi in a video."

He reached for her face and kissed her—hard. Marcy made a
mewing sound and pulled away. "Our mother of God. I'm sorry."

"That's not going to help a thing!" yelled Marcy. She rubbed
her nose. "You're the only one that knows. I mean, the only adult.
My boyfriend and his friends duplicated the video and they have
been passing it around, saying I wanted to make it, which isn't
altogether untrue. But I never intended for other people to see
it."

"Marcy, Marcy."

"I'm right here."

"Oh, Marcy."

"You sound like my dad."

He was still thinking how fleshy her lips felt against his, like
the inside of a plum, when she started hiking. He shook himself
out of his reverie and fell in beside her. They took turns slipping
between the small crevices.

"Marcy, we all make mistakes. That's why God gave his son
to us—that's why Jesus died on the cross, so our sins would be
forgiven." Although even as he spoke he was incredulous. His

Marcy naked on video?

"What about your sins?" asked Marcy.

"I am also human. I make mistakes. Here, sit." Father Tiko crouched down and tugged Marcy's hand, pulled her onto a decomposing log, the sides crumbling with chunks of wood. He looked at his shoes, noted how they rounded his feet like two squashes poking from the end of his toes; he wondered how his students clomped about in them every day. He was crafting his words. He wanted Marcy to feel he was trustworthy, so that she could release herself to the act of forgiveness. And he hadn't forgotten the kiss. She would need to forgive him before they returned to Aurora. That's where his mind was moored when she screamed.

It sounded as if a damp rag was stuffed inside her mouth. She screamed again and the air around him seemed to lift. Her voice rang in his ear. He shot up and looked to the place beside him: she was gone. He saw Marcy's jacket, feet spinning behind her, her hands tight balls. Father Tiko didn't have more than a moment. Something snarled at him. He flipped around. There was a cheetah, its jagged incisors oozing with saliva; it stood one foot over Father Tiko on a large, flat boulder, its tawny fur marked with stripes. "Run, Father!" Marcy screamed somewhere ahead of him. He did not pause. He took to the trail.

He ran, punching the air with his arms, swinging his fists, his new shoes slipping. If he'd been a cartoon, smoke would have wafted behind him. He felt the animal, nearly smelled its stink, its long slender legs bounding just a foot behind him, its small rounded head ready to pounce. Father Tiko scrambled past thin-necked trees. Somewhere Marcy stood in safety. She'd survived Hunted Trails before, although surely such a beast had never chased her!

He felt the pain of his injury before the cheetah's paw heaved through the air, its stout claws digging into his new jeans. The muscles of the beast pressed against him, the back of his own leg vicious and searing. "My God!" Blood seeped through his pants in fat strips. He continued sprinting in a place that felt more and more foreign. How much penance could he say for bringing Marcy here? Would any amount be adequate? His heart, quick and fierce, pummeled in his chest.

"Up here!" The voice was familiar. It took a minute to place it: Marcy. He looked in the direction of the voice and panted, only saw the rocky path before him. Then noticed her nestled in the bend of a tree.

He pumped his arms faster and circled the tree where Marcy sat in safety. The trunk seemingly grew taller as he sped around it, whittling a path. If he hesitated for a second upon reaching for the closest limb, the beast could easily pounce and maul him to death. His breath seemed to be failing him, light and airy, it dribbled out of his mouth, igniting a pain in his gut, burning his lungs. He waited too long. A pink blur zoomed out of the sky, yelling, "Ah ha!"

He prepared for the final pain, and glanced over his shoulder. It was Marcy. She straddled the cheetah, knees pressed into the animal's stomach. Her arms whipped in quick arcs. She wrestled with the beast while it bore up on its back legs, front legs in the air, pawing at wind; her hands dove into the black-striped fur. Father Tiko noticed that her fists were bloody and a slippery red mess fell into a pile at her suspended feet. He watched her squeeze the animal's head, the silver glimmer of a blade pointed in her fist. She dug the knife into its neck. The beast tipped to its side, its chest rising in rapid waves, its coat matted and wet, a blanket of red spewing forth. Marcy's own stylish fringed boots toed with blood. She leaned on her side, panting. "I saved you, Father," she grinned. "I saved the life of a priest." Red slashes smudged Marcy's face, her jeans speckled with thick, sticky clumps.

He put his own hand to his heart for some immediate sign of life.

"We're going to have to pay a fine," chirped Marcy. "You aren't supposed to kill the animals, but I didn't have a choice. You were going to be a goner," she said, using the sleeve of her jacket to push strands of hair from her mouth.

He found his voice. "Thank you, Marcy O'Connor."

She stood, wiped her hands on her jeans. "Jeez, I'm a mess. I know there's a public restroom around her somewhere. Can I see the map?"

Father Tiko felt around the inside of his jacket for his shirt pocket. He handed the folded brochure to Marcy. She opened the map, her fingerprints making red blotches on the paper.

"Just a mile or more that a way." She pointed with her elbow. "I knew we should have stayed in the beginner's section. No one's prepared for the animals the first time." She patted Father Tiko's shoulder. "It's okay," she told him.

He was in no position to question her sense of direction. When she started walking, he followed her.

"I know that the Church teaches us that life is precious," said Marcy, "and while I know I sinned when *you* made that video of me and Candace, I know that our lives will be blessed by God." It sounded so rehearsed. Marcy pulled up the collar of her jacket. Father Tiko began to shiver and pulled his hat down over his ears. "That safety you spoke of earlier? I can feel it right here." Marcy patted her chest.

Father Tiko felt tired. The chase. Her confession. It had happened so quickly he almost *could* believe that he had videotaped Marcy without her clothes, dancing and kissing a classmate. He placed one foot in front of the other, watched the pink of Marcy's jacket fall farther and farther away. He could still go to confession. It was not too late, not yet. He had friends; they'd tell him what to do before the accusations flew and the media became involved.

Every step felt weighted, each one taking him closer to a new reality he couldn't dare name. He moved forward, tried to gather himself when he heard it.

A deep guttural growl; it spooked the hair in his ears, pinched his toes and groin. Father Tiko looked to his left. A grizzly bear, over seven feet tall, clumsily moved toward him and erupted in a long-limbed roar. This time he knew what to do. He felt the wind in his thinning hair as he blazed past Marcy's form. The trees multiplied, flooded out, heavy with coldness and space. He felt the thrill. This was what Hunted Trails was all about. Humanness splintered his bones. Here Father Tiko was just like any other living being facing nature, and that was the person he would soon become.

# Nourishment

$S$cott phones the night before the wake. The butcher has not spoken to him for two years and his son's voice sounds like an apparition. After they discuss the plans for his wife's burial, his son interrupts him. "You should know I got married." The butcher wants to say it's sudden, and ask how well Scott knows the girl.

"Well, you've always done things your way," says the butcher.

"All you need to say is congratulations. Nothing more." Scott tells him they'll be in at noon and makes a point to say that the purpose for the visit is to pay respects to his mother.

The day before his son's arrival, the butcher washes coffee cups and puts away the tinfoil-wrapped dishes brought by his wife's friends. He is not looking forward to seeing his son. There will be fights. No matter how hard he might try, he knows there will be fights. While the butcher attended school until the twelfth grade, Scott had spent the last seven years working on a Ph.D. in astronomy, peering through telescopes and looking at the sky. But what do the stars matter? Even the butcher knows they are dead, light-years away. How do stars nourish people? They are only visible at night, during a time when most people were asleep. It is the butcher who can recite every cut on a cow blindfolded, just by the feel of the meat in his bare hands. He can wield the sharpest blades and fail to harm a fly, if need be.

The wind whips around outside the house the butcher once shared with his wife, and far off he hears the trilling of a wind chime. He steps out onto the front porch, blinks up at the sky, while a handful of marbles wink back. With time, the butcher would grow accustomed to the silence of the bungalow. His wife, he imagines, is in a better place than this. He breathes the crisp air and he thinks soon there will be snow and ice to combat during his drive to work. The furnace will need to be checked and his wife won't be there for any of it. He'll go it alone. If his wife were here she'd be talking about the neighbors, the ladies at church. Mindless chatter. The funeral itself will be an endless barrage of stories and hugs and he will have to pretend to be appreciative. He will act as if he knows the people who attend, as if their wishes of support mean something. To his wife, maybe it means something. To him, it is a bother.

This is before he meets Natalie, his son's wife.

Truth be told, he knew about the wedding last year. His wife had told him she was going, even gave him the option of attending the reception at the Ramada in Champaign. He had batted the idea around for a while, but his wife had taken ill a few days prior and Scott and his bride ultimately ended up at the courthouse, which to the butcher seemed easier to disregard.

Good God, the butcher thinks the following morning when he answers the door and sees Natalie standing there with an arm around his son. She leans forward and pecks both of his cheeks, then uses her thumb to wipe one of her kisses away. "I'm sorry. Look what I've done to your father, Scott."

"Ah, he won't mind. As long as you arrive at work on time and don't use too much bleach when you clean. That's the mistake I made."

The butcher takes Natalie's bag from her hand and ushers them inside. "It was your first week. I wanted to show you the right way to do it." He grits his teeth. "Who do you think paid for the hour we had to close Komo's because of the fumes?" They shuffle into the living room and sit on the faded corduroy couch. The carpeting is gray. On the wall is a framed picture of the three of them taken years ago. In the photo his wife is healthy and jovial, sitting beside the butcher. Scott is in front of them, a mouth full of braces. The butcher stares at the photo, time momentarily halted. It is as if he is looking at a still of someone else's life.

"I was thirteen, Dad. I didn't do it on purpose and I never did it again." Scott turns to Natalie, "He didn't talk to me for five weeks."

"Two," says the butcher.

Natalie faces him and speaks. "You stopped speaking to your son?" The butcher feels as if he's been scolded. His face reddens and his stomach flips and somersaults. How had his son convinced this woman to marry him? Petite with wavy hair the color of sand, her small hands tap the butcher's knee as if testing his reflexes. "Shame on you."

The butcher swallows. "I wasn't the best father." His words plummet in the air, hanging there like the glass baubles on the hallway chandelier.

"Don't be so generous," says Scott. He places an arm around Natalie and pulls her close, kisses her cheek.

The butcher can't recall the last time he yearned for anything, felt it so intensely it reverberated beneath his skin. But he feels that moment now.

The butcher curls his hands into fists and hopes for one thing: he wishes he was his son.

In the two days since his wife has passed he has not slept through the night. It is as if his sixty-eight-year-old body were no longer interested in hiding in dreams and remaining still. He wakes several times and sometimes gives up on sleep altogether, lumbering into the living room and turning on all the lights, watching television until the lamplight dulls in comparison to the vibrance outside. He knew one of them would go first. It isn't a complete surprise, but he does miss her voice, the vanilla-scented soap she used in the bath, the way she patted his back each morning before he left for work.

Now he remains motionless in his bed for fear Scott and Natalie, his guests, might hear his fitfulness. And then the feeling arrives. Sudden and vicious like the sickening rise in the belly after a night of heavy drinking or the sour taste of old meat. He grows hot all over as if a match has been taken to his pajama bottoms, and just as quickly, the heat in his stomach subsides. His toes tingle and he wiggles them.

"Are you trying to get fresh with me in your folks' house?" says the voice.

The butcher squints into the darkness. He can just make out the close form of the walls. A pesky coil juts into his thigh—he is in the guest bedroom with its old mattress. He shoots up, turns his hands over, pats his now firm chest and grabs his biceps— muscles that long ago faded are suddenly solid and bulging. The physique of a twenty-nine-year-old man.

The butcher is inside his son's body.

He glances at her. Natalie wears a dark gown of some sort, her bare arms roping toward him. The butcher darts out of the bed and into the kitchen. She follows behind, her hands swishing against the sides of her gown. "Scott? Everything okay?"

The butcher fills a glass with water from the tap and stands in the moonlight looking out at the neighbors' yard. There is a rusted play set with two swings creaking in the frigid air. Scott and the neighbors' kids are the same age. Years ago the same uneven rings and rusty-chain swings once belonged to them. Nowadays, he never sees anyone playing on the play set, yet it remains standing, a dull contraption groaning on the blue-frosted grass. Natalie's bare feet smack the linoleum. She places a hand around his waist. "It's going to be okay." She hugs him from behind, and her breasts press through her thin nightgown. "Let's go back to bed," she whispers. "We don't want to wake your father."

Yes. He nods, lets her take his hand. They pass his bedroom door and he hesitates. Who is inside his room? Has he died? Is he now floating inside his son's body while all his evil deeds are counted? In the guest room, Natalie's skin embraces his body, the dull warmth of a lamp that won't burn out. She snuggles into his neck and the last thing the butcher recalls is her breathing, "I love you." And he thinks: maybe I have not been such a bad man.

*H*e wakes in his own bedroom, more rested than ever, as if he's slept for a lifetime and a half. The butcher rubs at his eyes, stretches his arms over his head and feels for the muscles—they are gone. His body has returned—bone and loose skin, a bag of fat around his middle; he is somewhat relieved. A dream, he reasons. Something that doesn't matter.

The butcher tosses back the blankets and fits his feet into slippers. He patters off to the kitchen where he scratches the hair on his chest and scoops coffee into the filter. He fills the pot with cold water and watches steam well up on the window behind the coffee maker. Fiddling with the waist of his pajama pants, he steers off to the bathroom where he brushes his teeth and splashes his face with water. When he returns to the kitchen, Natalie is sitting at the table cupping a mug. "I hope you don't mind. I helped myself."

The butcher gestures the thought away. "Make yourself at home," he says. He takes out the milk and sugar and fixes his coffee at the counter, his back to her. What if she knows about his dream? He hadn't even considered it. Scott is her husband—of course she is familiar with everything about him.

"You didn't sleep well," says the butcher.

"I slept fine," says Natalie. "In fact, I haven't slept so soundly in months. It was like I was in some sleep coma."

"I figured you must not have slept well, up so early and all."

"No, Scott's the late sleeper. It's worked out, though."

The butcher concurs. He doesn't want her to stop talking. "More?" he holds up the pot, refills her mug. He watches her lips as she speaks.

"Scott and I were in the same physics class first semester of college. Guess who ended up with the higher grade?"

He shrugs.

"Me! We studied the same things. Somehow I edged him out. I like to tease him about that."

The butcher's face breaks into a grin. "Like his old man. Neither of us likes to lose."

"Ah," she says, "now I know where he gets it."

This woman is maddeningly charming.

*T*hey have made plans to go to the cemetery and finish the arrangements. Piling into Scott's foreign compact, the butcher insists on sitting in the back seat, his knees huddled to his chest. "Are you sure you're okay?" asks Natalie. His eyes fix on her face.

The glorious openness of it all.

"This is great." His toes begin to prickle and numb and he scrunches them inside his shoes. The butcher amicably holds his knees, waits for Scott to say something. Instead, his son turns on the radio and the sound from the speakers pierces the butcher's ears. "Scott! The music is too dang loud!"

Natalie is the one to turn it off altogether. "Sorry," she says.

"You're fine, Natalie." The butcher slams his fist onto the seat. It slaps the vinyl and sounds like spit hitting an empty soda can.

"Give it up, Dad. What have I done now that's so terrible?"

"See? That. Right there. Your smarmy attitude."

"See?" Scott turns to Natalie. "This is my dad, the real guy, not some sugar-puffed version. He's as much of a jerk as ever. I don't know how Mom lived with him as long as she did." Scott blasts the volume on the music and the reverberations wave through the tiny car.

Natalie flicks it off again. "Stop it!"

"You blow everything out of proportion," says the butcher. "Your mother could have left if she'd wanted to. I didn't hold a gun to her head."

"You might as well have. You can't do a thing but chop meat. If she'd left you'd never have survived."

"That'd please you, wouldn't it?" he says.

"Scott, please," says Natalie.

"Nat, I'm trying. Nothing has changed."

The car turns into Our Lady of Perpetual Rest and slowly motors past tall sweeping statures of saints and angels, sloping green hills and gray trees whose lingering leaves are fingered with bits of gold and red. Scott parks the car next to a water pipe where two older women in trench coats and plastic bonnets fill watering cans. Scott and Natalie tumble out of the compact. Natalie holds the front seat forward and the butcher staggers to his feet. He hops from one foot to the next, and the blood gradually returns to them. Natalie places an arm around both him and Scott and they walk to the empty gravesite, standing side by side. The ground where his wife will rest has already been cleared and a bright green tarp covers the rectangular opening in the earth. A pile of dirt stands to the side. His wife had known how to handle Scott. But to him, his son is a mystery.

When he sharpens the cleavers and rolls a beef leg out of the refrigerator, he can tell which cuts are top round with his eyes clamped shut. He is the one who directs the knife to saw and slice and carve, attempts just the right amount of marbling, stacking the pieces onto Styrofoam trays. He has spent hours behind the butcher counter, his hands coated in oily blood, surrounded by death. Yet here, at the cemetery, he is at a loss. And it is the cycle of his emotions that surprises him most. Last night he dreamed he was in bed with his daughter-in-law. Is he losing his mind?

Tears spring from his eyes and he is shocked that something so warm dribbles with such weightlessness. He is becoming an old man. Natalie hugs him. "She misses you, too. I'm certain of it." His brow relaxes with her voice and he wipes his face with his fingers. Scott pulls the car closer while Natalie hooks an arm around the butcher's shoulders. She slips into the back seat with him and keeps one arm around him the entire drive home.

"You've been a good provider," says Scott. "A fine dad." At home, his son lifts the blankets over the butcher's legs. It sounds like he is speaking underwater. Why is he telling him this? It doesn't mean a thing. The butcher wants them to leave. Give him his house and his knives and his cutting board. Leave him with his silence.

He can hear them whispering in their room, about him most likely, and the fact that he is nearly senile. Less than a mile away is a retirement home. Scott can drop him off there, sell the house, and take his beautiful wife on a European cruise. If anyone deserved it, she did.

He descends into sleep, confident it's a better place to be. Quick warmth invades his body, a tingling like tiny bells dangling over his head. He hears breathing first, then feels her weight beside him. Natalie is rolled up, her fists in front of her, the sides of her palms just brushing the coarse hairs on his chest. He doesn't need to flex a single muscle. He knows where he is and why he is here. It is his wife who has placed him beside Natalie—she always knew what he needed before he ever did.

His chest burns for the woman he married and the time they had in their house, the meals they shared, the nights they passed. The butcher's throat tightens with the definite conclusion of all of this. He recalls his wife while Natalie breathes next to him. He nudges Natalie's chin. She smells musky, like the dust balls hidden beneath the dresser and nightstand. He lifts her head and slides his elbow under her neck. While her eyes are closed he holds her hair up to his nose. Cinnamon? Nutmeg? So familiar.

"Love? Scott?" She buries her face into the base of his neck and swallows.

"It's me," he says. The butcher lifts her face to his, her head wobbly in his hands. Her eyelids flutter open, and then close. He leans in and presses his lips against hers for minutes or an hour; no amount of time would ever be enough. But he is grateful for his one moment, even while waiting for it to be taken away.

# Girls Who Do It

$T$he original list was comprised of seventeen names, one for each year of their short lives. All kinds of boys and men were on that list and they weren't just from St. Boniface. Andy Lemulson was first. He played second string on the basketball team, had pretty good skin, and was around six-feet tall. Hala, Cindy, and Irene had placed him first on the list because he'd dated a senior last year and everyone at St. Boniface knew they were doing it. Hala, Cindy, and Irene needed something of their own to be good at, like the members of the school band with their red polyester pants and matching berets.

They met at Irene's house to plan.

Irene was afraid her mother would hear their discussion even though she was watching *Jeopardy* and yelling out the answers. Just to be safe, they had on WKCO during a stretch of U2 songs.

They determined the approach would be complicated with the first four or five boys. After that people would know about them. Then it would be easy. "*Seventeen* always says how boys love to have the pressure taken off," said Cindy.

Irene started pacing, wringing her fingers. "Shh! I think I hear my mother."

"Chill out, Irene," said Hala. "Nothing's gonna happen." Hala turned up the volume on the radio. "There."

"Are you kidding?" asked Irene. "We're talking about asking boys to have intercourse!"

"Don't call it that," said Cindy. "It sounds like you're talking about some experiment or something."

"Well, isn't it?"

"Did you think they'd just read our minds and come up to us?" said Cindy.

"Listen, Irene. If you're not into this, just tell Cindy and me now and we'll do this on our own. There have always been three of us but it can just as easily be two." She softened her tone and told Irene to sit down, patting the quilt on the bed. "Now listen. We're going to write them letters. Nobody writes letters anymore, so we will. We'll write up a general letter that we can all use. We'll tell them where to meet us, what time, all the things you'd usually talk about on the phone or in person, except we'll also tell them what they'll get out of a meeting with us."

"Does that mean we'll have to call them to remind them of their appointments?" asked Irene.

"No, they'll remember. We'll write the letter in a way that they won't forget," said Hala.

Hala raised her mug of Hawaiian Punch and the other two followed suit. "To us."

Before they ended that first meeting, Hala unlatched her red leather purse and pulled out a box of Trojans. She handed both Irene and Cindy four of the square packets. "Nobody wants to get pregnant or diseased—make sure you use these every time."

Irene, the most devout Catholic of the three, stared at Hala's open palm.

"Come on, Irene," said Hala.

"It's going to be great, you'll see," said Cindy.

Hala split open one of the packages and pulled out the snatch of rubber. It looked like a little Mexican hat. Hala jumped up and grabbed Irene's Cabbage Patch doll and lifted up its dress so one leg poked out. Hala unrolled the condom over the doll's leg. "See? It's that simple."

"Poor Darleen!" said Irene, who grabbed the doll from Hala's hands.

The following week they agreed to meet at Cindy's house. By then, they'd all have lost their virginity to Andy Lemulson.

Cindy told Irene over the telephone how she passed her letter to Andy Lemulson during British literature. Their teacher was reviewing for an exam over *To the Lighthouse* and Andy gave Cindy a puzzled look when she placed it on top of his notebook. He unfolded the stationery, read the contents of the letter, and then quickly folded it. He didn't lift his eyes from his notes during the rest of class. But he was in the pump room of St. Boniface pool on Saturday afternoon when the pool was leased out to the local age group team. Cindy had laid out a Snoopy beach towel and had brought the Trojans from Hala. When Andy arrived, Cindy was perched on the towel in a turquoise push-up bra and matching velvet panties.

From the pump room, Cindy heard the pop of the starter's gun and the crowd cheering. They started kissing and when Andy pushed his tongue in Cindy's mouth, she started to feel woozy and warm.

"Did it hurt?" asked Irene.

"There was a quick pain when he pushed so I let Andy do most of the work. Afterwards he gave me a ride home in his Malibu."

"Was that it?" asked Irene.

"Well, what more do you want?"

"Did he say anything when he dropped you off?"

"Sure," said Cindy. "He said he'd see me at school."

$\mathcal{H}$ala told Irene how she met Andy at the forest preserve, mimicking one of her stepfather's porns where the couple goes at it in the woods. She whispered little things while she and Andy Lemulson did it: *You feel like a rocket ready for take-off, Fly with me,* and *Big daddy!* Andy erupted with a howl that sent two squirrels running. While she and Andy flattened the heads of wild mushrooms and crunched sticks between kneecaps, Hala told him, "You are the best ever."

"Well, was he?" asked Irene.

"Irene," Hala blew the air out of her mouth and shook her head. "Just because you say something doesn't mean you actually mean it."

"I know *that*," said Irene.

It was Tuesday and Irene still hadn't given Andy her letter. That night, while sitting in bed she was thinking of quitting the whole thing. She'd never dated. She'd kissed one boy on a dare and her mother was always telling her how difficult it was to be a single mother. "There is no greater cross to bear than raising a child alone," she frequently said. "Your father didn't plan on leaving us, but God had other arrangements."

Irene had nearly talked herself out of it when she flipped through her quote book, the one with the positive sayings she had been collecting since the fourth grade. It was this quote by Helen

Keller that changed everything: "Life is either a daring adventure or nothing at all." That did it. She was tired of burning omelets during home economics and staying up all night to prepare for science exams. Most Friday nights were spent with her mom, sharing a double pepperoni. Irene wanted more and punctured the air with her fist. Wouldn't it be nice to feel someone's skin against her? To be held, so sweetly and spoken to lovingly? Copulating was natural. A hundred years ago, at her age, she would already be married, toddlers scratching at her legs. What was so evil about biology? She decided to make her life something and Andy Lemulson would be the start of it.

The following day, Irene told her mom she was staying after to tutor a lower-track chemistry student. When classes ended that afternoon, she prepared. Irene typed her letter to Andy in the computer lab and used a fourteen-point font so he would not miss a word. She walked past the gym where basketballs reverberated off the waxed floor and Andy practiced with the rest of the team.

Inside the girls' locker room, Irene brushed her hair, rinsed her mouth out with water, and inspected her teeth. She went out to the parking lot in search of Andy's maroon Chevy Malibu. The rear passenger door was unlocked, so after she unfolded the note beneath the wipers, she slid onto the floor of his car. A vanilla air freshener hung from the mirror and just a few wadded up Kleenexes spotted the floor. Irene took that as a positive sign. She found a chemistry book under the seat, so she stretched out and began studying.

Irene waited on the floor of Andy's car until she heard the key in the lock and the front seat smashed against her head.

She repeated Helen Keller's quote to herself, scrunched her fists and waited until she heard Andy rustle the paper. He was reading the letter. The car door was still open and the edgy briskness of March sprung up under her uniform skirt. Irene took a deep breath and popped her head up. "Hi! I'm Irene."

He jumped, turned around, and let out a little squeak.

"Sorry," she said.

His words rushed out in a flurry. "What the heck are you doing here?"

"That letter's from me." Of course by now he'd been with Cindy and Hala. He knew the routine. He looked down at the letter in his hand. Irene said, "I have a deadline—" She hated that part. If she had planned it better she could have just slipped the letter in his locker rather than watch him read it. He stared at her for several minutes, perhaps trying to figure out if it was worth it or not. Then he slammed the car door and started the ignition.

In the letter, Irene had asked him to meet her at the Motel 6 on Reitz Avenue, next to Jewel Foods. He took the turns quickly. Irene wasn't about to lose her virginity in the back seat of some car. She'd taken out money from her savings account and handed Andy thirty dollars for a room with a double bed and cable television.

The whole thing was awkward. As soon as he shut the door to the room, Andy Lemulson started taking off his clothes until he was standing there in his undershorts with a little bulge in the front. Irene leaned against the door; he'd already hopped into bed.

"Come 'ere," he said. She thought of her friends, thought about herself. Who was she, standing in a hotel room before a nearly naked boy? The third time, Andy called her name sharply and she went to him, sat on the tippy tip of the bed, tucking her hands beneath her knees. He pushed her onto her back and began unbuttoning her blouse. What if she became pregnant? What would her mother say? She stared at the water stain on the ceiling. "No! Stop!" Irene jumped up. "I'm sorry. It was a mistake." She tucked in her blouse.

"But you asked me here," said Andy. "You wrote the letter—just like the other two."

"I'm sorry. Please." Irene pressed up against the door, her
palm fixed on the knob.

"Freak," he said. "Fuckin' freak."

Irene left Andy money for gas and started on the three-mile
walk home. She was thankful for the dark cape of evening, the
soft glow of the streetlights. When she returned to her house,
she found her mom in the kitchen, placing chunks of frozen
fried chicken into a baking dish.

"Have a good day, hon?" asked her mom.

"Sure."

"It's almost the weekend," her mother continued. "If you've
made some new friends you could have them over."

"No thanks." Irene unzipped her coat. Hala and Cindy were
the only friends she had. She went into the bathroom where she
undressed and remained under the showerhead until the water
stung her skin a deep shade of pink.

The following evening they exchanged their stories at
Cindy's house while listening to "Valerie Loves Me" on WKCO
over an open box of banana twins. Cindy and Irene couldn't
believe Hala had taken Andy outdoors. "He was an animal! Simply crazy!" said Hala. This quieted Cindy and Irene. Cindy rustled
with the cellophane wrapper of another dessert snack.

They questioned Irene: "You really sat in the back of Andy
Lemulson's car during basketball practice?"

"It was fun," murmured Irene.

"I'll say," said Cindy, "But tiring—all that breathing and
grunting."

"That's a good thing. You want them to put some effort forth. It shouldn't just be like a walk along the beach," said Hala.

This was something Irene could speak about. "You know that intercourse increases not only your heart rate but also the blood flow to your brain. It can help you think better, improve your breathing, circulation—even your skin."

Her friends rolled their eyes. "Puhleez."

At the end of the evening, Hala and Irene walked home together. Hala had a way of holding herself as if she was constantly aware of her own beauty. Just sharing the sidewalk with her, Irene felt dumpy. "It's just me, Irene. You can be honest. You hated it, right?"

"Well, I think it was Andy," said Irene. "We didn't click."

Hala stopped walking and held up a hand. "I'm going to do you a favor. I'll take your place. You still write the letters and make appointments with the guys, but I'll show up on your behalf."

"But then you'll be with the same boy twice."

"Not really. I'll tell them I'm there on your account, that when they talk, they've got to say they've been with you."

The moon bent high and full. They crossed the street, porch lights dotting the rows of houses. A car sped past. Irene's hands were sweaty. Before she could ask her question, Hala answered: "Because we're friends and we do things for each other." Irene tugged on the sleeves of her jacket and buried her hands inside the openings. She didn't know how to respond and chose not to.

Lorenzo Mattio was second on the list. They'd all sat next to Lorenzo at some time in grade school. In the seventh grade he had won the state science fair for his experiment studying bacterial growth in non-pasteurized apple cider. His father owned a pizzeria downtown and Lorenzo was in mostly honors classes, olive-skinned with brisk stubble at his chin.

Hala told Cindy and Irene the following Wednesday how Lorenzo had shown up carrying a box of chocolate caramels, wearing a navy suit and plaid tie. Hala was already there, positioned inside the funhouse dressed in a chartreuse and black-sequined one-piece. "He might have been a virgin," Hala had admitted. "But he woke up quickly and held on with some kind of endurance. All those years of his mother's tortellini salad."

Cindy and Lorenzo did it in the women's restroom on the fourth floor of the university library. At one point, she told Irene, she hung from the stall dividers, one hand on each side, wiggling her hips in a circle and then kicking into a handstand. Lorenzo's eyes widened and Cindy invented her trademark position. Cindy told Irene that Lorenzo passed out with his head underneath the sink. She had to slap his scruffy cheeks with the back of her hand, and when he woke his face was white and clammy.

Irene had always thought Lorenzo was cute. She had been invited to his third-grade birthday party when he received a beagle pup. He let each of his guests hold the pup and he didn't even time how long each of them held it. Irene also admired Lorenzo's scientific work. Years ago, when Lorenzo beat Irene at the regional semi-finalist science fair, she'd been angry, mostly envious. But when Irene finally made her way over to Lorenzo's project, she was thoroughly impressed by his careful attention to detail. His poster explained fermentation quite clearly. He had also created a diorama of the pasteurization process and had filled paper cups with free samples of apple cider.

Irene slipped the letter to Lorenzo in his locker and waited behind the Motel 6 dumpster; she watched him hunch next to the empty swimming pool. She had the urge to talk to him—ask him about his family, his classes, whether he was reading anything interesting—when Hala arrived. Lorenzo seemed surprised to see Hala, but he looked pleased nonetheless, rubbing his hands together as if he was preparing to knead pizza dough.

It was obvious during the Wednesday evening after they had each been with Lorenzo that both Hala and Cindy were attracted to him. Hala said Lorenzo wanted to take her to meet his family in Naples, Italy.

"He wasn't serious," said Cindy.

"How do you know?" asked Hala.

"Well," responded Cindy. "I can't stop thinking about doing it with him."

"Ah, the obsessive lover," said Hala.

"I'm not obsessed, I'm interested," said Cindy. Hala and Cindy both rated Lorenzo fives, and sat there glaring at one another. They didn't even ask Irene what her experience with him had been like. So she just chimed in, "Put me down for a five as well." On the way home, Cindy wanted to know what Irene thought about Lorenzo. "An animal," she blurted, "for sure."

Cindy agreed.

Irene grew cold. It was nearly June and while the air had become warm, Irene pulled out her winter sweaters from storage, wrapped her neck in wool scarves. Her head did not feel right unless it was confined within a scratchy knit cap. Still, her teeth had the inclination to chatter, bump against one another. Each day after school, she returned to her bedroom where she read textbooks—biology, chemistry, physics, pharmacology, and physiology. Dense things that her eyes slowly traversed.

When Irene stepped into the kitchen for a glass of water one night, her mother asked, "Are you feeling okay?"

"I'm fine. Busy studying," she responded. Her mother had been watching *Wheel of Fortune* and called Irene over to the couch.

She pressed a hand against Irene's forehead and the back of her neck.

"You don't have a fever."

"I have a lot of homework." Irene edged back toward her room.

"Don't spend all your time reading. Have you made any new friends at school?"

"A few." She let the words slide down her chest.

"Well, keep trying," said her mother. "Anyone else would be better than *those* girls."

"They're starting to talk about us." Hala laughed freely. She turned on WKCO and sang a few lines from "Open Your Heart" by Madonna. She was in a buoyant mood. *The Cosby Show* was on TV and Irene's mother's cackle shot through the thin bedroom door.

Since Hala and Cindy had arrived, Irene's mother had opened the door twice without knocking, once to offer a bag of potato chips, the second, to hand them a pitcher of Kool-Aid. After the last interruption Irene jammed her desk chair under the door.

"All right!" Cindy clapped her hands overhead. Irene remained motionless, a stocking cap pulled over her ears, a scarf at her neck. "Hey Irene, they say you're an easy lay, that you don't do much, just let them go at it," said Hala.

Irene shrugged. "You both know I'm more interested in the process—intercourse releases epinephrine and other endorphins, both of which elevate mood and temperament."

"Hello! Haven't you been listening to us?" asked Cindy. "You should try the top."

Hala interrupted Cindy. "They say you, Cindy, have no rhythm."

"Who said that?" Cindy was immediately crestfallen, her tiny mouth flipped downwards.

"I've been talking to some basketball players in study hall. The boys like the letters, though, and I've heard positive things about your underwear."

"What have they been saying about you?" asked Cindy.

"Well, they aren't going to say those things to my face. That's my game, not theirs." Irene had heard that Hala talked to boys the whole time and yelled so loudly that some boys heard ringing in their ears.

While they continued to meet each week to discuss their experiences, it felt to Irene as if something great had shifted. Hala was sleeping with the guys on Irene's behalf and each time she sat beside her friends, Irene cushioned herself with a pad of lies. Who were these girls? Irene had chosen them as friends, right? Or they had chosen her. It hadn't mattered before. Now it did.

After Lorenzo Mattio, there was Philip Dans, who ran for junior class president and Kurt, the Quik Fill attendant that slung a Valvoline cap low over his eyes. Georgio Zissamopolous was number five; he was the Greek chef at the all-night diner. The seventy-four-year-old pool manager from the YMCA became number six. He had difficulty remaining erect and the girls ended up just hugging him while he kissed their necks.

There was only one who refused.

*T*he final weeks of school arrived. They crossed off names. Irene was careful to show neither too much nor too little interest in the boys chosen each week. She wore her winter coat over two sweaters, a scratchy cap drawn tightly on top of her ears. Instead of taking notes, she began drawing muscles and ropes of connective tissues during class lectures. She saw the inside of each organ, the train of each vein, its slick red vessel. She stopped asking questions in class and slipped into her own mind, unaware of where she was.

"Irene! Irene!" Cindy and Hala ran up beside her as she exited St. Boniface. "We've been calling you for a hundred years," said Cindy.

"Oh. I didn't hear you." She really didn't; she tried to ignore Hala and Cindy and often she did so without even realizing it.

They flanked her on either side and walked home with her. "Are you avoiding us?" asked Hala. "It almost seems like you're embarrassed to hang around with us."

"I've had a lot going on," she responded.

Cindy placed an arm around her shoulder. "We're best friends! You can lean on us." Cindy tipped her head onto Irene's coat, and then just as quickly moved away from her. "What's with the winter gear?"

"I'm cold."

"You're weird," said Cindy.

"What she means is if we can help with something you know we will," said Hala.

Moving about Irene's kitchen, they looked for food. Irene grabbed a bag of unopened pretzels and Cindy found half a box of sugar wafers. They sat on the couch and munched. Hala brought up Leonard Frye; he would be number eleven. Leonard Frye with his disfigured nose and curling hair. They ended the whole thing with him.

"We don't need him. I don't want to look at that nose," said Cindy.

Irene no longer cared about much. She was wearing long underwear under her uniform and had stopped showering. Her hair had grown thick and dull with oil. She spoke up on Leonard's behalf. "The poor guy has had over ten surgeries since the sixth grade. Why don't you leave him alone?"

Hala glared at her. "The thing about Leonard is that we can give him something. We've all known him for so long. We've all felt badly for his condition, here's our chance to give him something to remember."

Irene saw Leonard's zigzagged nose, one nostril flattened nearly to his lip, his round collared shirts just grazing the ends of his hair. She shivered, thought about the double-ply socks in her dresser drawers, the mittens just a few feet away.

"Plus, if we change our minds now, they'll all hear about it." Hala focused on each girl. "You don't think they watch us presenting our letters into the hands of these boys? They are looking over our shoulders at every moment. There's no backing away."

"I guess," said Cindy. "We have reputations."

Irene spoke up. "Just leave Leonard Frye alone. Choose somebody else."

"Like who, Irene? Who are you interested in getting close to?" Hala's voice was laced with coolness. Irene shrugged, her teeth chattered.

Two days later, Cindy borrowed her father's Chevy. She and Hala stood outside Irene's locker and each grabbed one of her arms, led her to the St. Boniface parking lot and pulled her into the car. They drove into an unincorporated area of town. It was a deserted road with overgrown weeds, rusted cans, and crumpled sale papers. Together they watched Leonard get off the bus and Cindy idled slowly behind, the Chevy encapsulated in a cloud of sooty dust.

"Hey Len!" said Hala, hanging out the window. "Wanna ride?"

He tugged the straps of his backpack. "No thanks."

"Then we'll walk with you. It's not like you don't know us or anything." Hala threw open the door and hopped out. Irene waited for Cindy to stop the car before she stepped onto the gravel.

The four of them started walking. Hala and Cindy on Leonard's left, Irene on his right. Irene was the same height as Leonard. The webbed snow fences still twisted along the road. "Are your classes going well?" asked Cindy.

"I guess as well as can be expected. I'm going to apply for early admission to the University of Michigan."

"That's great," said Irene. "Biology?"

"Maybe. Science for sure, possibly genetics."

"Which one is your house?" asked Hala. Leonard pointed to the only house for miles; it was painted an eggshell blue and its gutters were peeling. "Do you think we could come in for a drink or something?" Hala wiped the back of her neck with her palm.

"I guess that'd be okay. I don't know what we have." Leonard fished into the neck of his shirt and pulled out a shoestring with a key dangling at its end. "It's a little messy. My brother's four."

"That's fine. We'll wait out here," said Irene.

He climbed up the steps and from behind the screen door Irene watched him pull three cans of soda from the refrigerator.

"Here." The girls sat on the porch steps and sipped the drinks while Leonard stood there, hands glued to his sides.

"Not thirsty, Len?" asked Hala. He shook his head. Branches held tightly-cupped buds, bits of green and red; the whirl of the highway spooled in the distance.

"Here we are," said Hala, placing her drink on the step. Irene watched Hala stand up, flick her hands on Leonard's shoulders and jerk him suddenly, pushing him flat against the porch floor. The top of his collarbone peeked from his jacket. The hottest day of the year and he didn't even break a sweat; his windbreaker remained zipped halfway. Irene marveled at his nose; it looked even more unusual surrounded by nothing. He looked off beyond them; his glazed eyes matched the faded ground. Hala leaned over Leonard and held his elbows over his head. He was bent at an awkward angle. "You're the best, Leonard," said Hala, half-singing. "We're stronger than you and we always will be." She tightened her fist and punched him right in the middle of the chest. Leonard started coughing, rolled to his side.

"Stop!" Irene tossed her can aside and dropped her body between Hala and the doubled-over Leonard. "Are you okay, Len?" He wiped at his nose, held his stomach. Irene squinted at Hala and Cindy. "I want Leonard. Let me be with him."

Hala laughed. "You haven't fucked a single guy, Irene. Not since the first time."

"She hasn't?" asked Cindy.

"You can listen," said Irene. "You can do whatever you have to for proof."

Hala shrugged. "Suit yourself. Go to town." She stepped back, leaned on the porch railing, stared.

He looked like a lost bird, twisted on his side. Irene kept waiting for him to protest or try to get up and get away. Cindy had left the car radio on and WKCO played a song by R.E.M. Irene could hear the music wafting over the baked road, the yellow haze lifting up around her. She didn't look at Hala or Cindy, but she could imagine their expressions.

"Hey, Leonard." Irene bent down beside him on the long wide porch. "It's me, Irene." She put her hands around his back and hugged him close, the way she might cradle an infant, tucking him into her breast.

# The Country of Women

Men shuffled down the aisles tight-fisting carts, wide-eyed at colorful boxes of cake mix and instant potatoes. The manager, in his purple silk-screened jacket, stood in as cashier and the check-out line snaked past the magazines. I filled my cart with orange juice, tomato soup, and a few other essentials and lined up behind Jerry Chimera. His farm was not too far from ours. I tipped my cap to him.

Howdy, he said.

Where's the cashier? I asked.

Jerry stood there, cheeks a mottled red, and shifted his portliness from one boot to the next. The guy in front of Jerry turned around, stared, and when I caught his eye he looked away, as if checking out the special on 7-Up. Jerry put a hand on my elbow and it struck me as a way I might touch Marlene if she was acting particularly odd. He lowered his voice and asked, When did you last hear from Marlene?

Where did—

Jerry flipped his palm up at me like a stop sign. He whispered, They're gone. All the women.

But——. There was nothing to say. I hadn't seen my wife in two days.

I took the long way home from the grocery store along the huddled buildings downtown. There was a closed sign outside the New Day Salon and the lights were out at the Fashion Junction. The streets were bustling with men. Young fathers who should have been walking their kids home from kindergarten instead led their oversized dogs on leashes and headed toward McCutter's for a drink. The ones closer to my age stomped in and out of Duds N' Suds with arms full of clean flannels, crumpled and unfolded.

What I now know is that they left in the middle of the night, wrapped slices of white bread in waxed paper, tucked flat-bottomed shoes in the waists of their pants, and tossed blankets over their limber backs. We men were sleeping, dreaming of goats and black soil.

That last night together my wife and I went to bed after the news; she closed her eyes during the sports segment. I kissed her cool cheek, told her I hoped she slept well. There were no harsh words. Later that night, she stood at the barn while I slept, gave her four Holsteins one last talking to; she whispered encouraging words, touched their felt-tipped ears with the very edges of her fingers. Perhaps she told them to befriend me. There was no warning of the women's departure, just an early fog, the caramelized leaves pale and dewy, and a somber gale tossing them to the ground in fistfuls. The morning after they disappeared I stood at the screen door in my blue socks, sipping a cup of coffee, looking out at the long flat land, the new shoots of winter wheat threading past the ground cover.

I could not recall any discord.

When I think of her slipping out from our bed of thirty-some years while my body remained heavy and unmoving, I wonder, Why didn't I wake? Did she sneak something into my evening coffee? Maybe they drugged all of us.

What I miss most are her morning sounds. Shuffling in the bathroom, water beating against her breasts while she showered, and later, her hard stream in the toilet. At night, her thick thighs against mine.

At first I thought Marlene had left to see her sister in Pittsburgh. I didn't tell anyone she was gone. I spent the following morning in the fields tilling around the wheat to break up the frost. The new crop needed to grow a good three inches before the cold weather set in. I gave Marlene's Holsteins their morning grain and sat alongside them for milking, my face near the warmth of their steamy udders, my thoughts fixed on Marlene. If she told anyone her plan, she probably told these gentle and slow-moving animals. When we left the city for the country, her only request was a barn with cows. That didn't surprise me. Marlene was like that—getting an idea in her head and sticking to it, although I had thought she wanted the cows for fresh cream.

Many mornings when Marlene was still here, I'd wake to an empty bed and after pulling on boots and coat, I'd step outside to find the doors of our barn open. She would be inside with her nightgown hiked up to her knees, just a scarf wrapped around her neck, hair pulled on top of her head. Marlene's body would be squeezed close to the cow, humming against her bottom lip while dawn moved in and the fierce sound of milk echoed in the metal pail. Steam rose from the cow's warmth and made wings of Marlene's hair.

I'd call her name several times before she responded and remembered me.

# The Country of Women

Marlene and I had our rough times, like when we first married. Only once did she attempt to leave. The kids were young—both under three and she had first started to put on weight. Her uniform black hair became interspersed with gray strands, like cracks that form along the ceiling of a settling house. We were living in the city and one evening I returned from my sales job to find her bruised suitcase packed and standing near the door. I found the kids in the playpen and followed the sound of guitars and a fiddle to our bedroom.

Marlene had turned the country station to the highest decibel and I worried she would permanently damage her eardrums. She was dressed in her wedding gown; it was zipped halfway and her back bulged in plump half-moons. The color on her toes was chipped and peeling and the sight of those tiny pretty toes made me pause. Marlene had her arms out in a circle in front of her, swaying her hips and turning around our bed as if it was an ornate water fountain centered in a ballroom. She didn't stop dancing even after I stepped in front of her. So I loosened my tie and shimmied up to her, slid underneath the circle of her arms and started moving right along with her.

Within four months we bid out of our lease and left for Mokena.

The cows were the first things in our marriage Marlene had asked for and I thought they would satisfy her. Really, I thought all was well between us. Our years together might not have been the life she imagined, but Marlene never told me otherwise. She never complained. We raised two good kids; we owned our house and had money in the bank. The only recent argument that circles my mind is a discussion we had weeks before she left. Marlene was going on about how the smallest cow didn't seem to be eating as much as the others. She must have asked me something about the health of this cow because she stopped talking mid-sentence and by the time I finished my banana bread and asked her to repeat herself, Marlene wouldn't respond. She didn't resume speaking for the rest of the evening. Finally, after a day of this silence, I followed her downstairs where she was ironing and I held her arms in my hands until she told me what was wrong. In a firm voice she said I didn't listen to her or show any interest in the cows. She barely glanced at me as she spoke. I told her she was being ridiculous. I repeated that twice.

Alone at home, I watched the cows in pasture, herded the four of them in for evening milking. Their bellies were full. I squatted beside them and took two teats in my hands; fierce white ricocheted in the bucket. I poured each full bucket into the bulk tank that refrigerated the milk until the dairy picked it up. Marlene had named the cows, but I could never keep their names straight. She called them her girls. It hadn't made any sense to me to try and make an animal human. Maybe with the kids grown she needed something to care for. I thought then about calling our two kids and telling them Marlene was missing along with the other women. They were adults now with families of their own. Ultimately I decided against it.

Sleep was the first thing I altered following Marlene's disappearance. I took to our bedroom and began sleeping in the middle of the day, when the September sun was at its most brilliant and I thought it could infuse my bones with its bright gleam. I woke at seven in the evening, dressed in dark woolens and made myself a sausage sandwich. I looked in on the girls, gently chewing in their respective sections of the barn. I imagine Marlene told the cows how she had made a mistake long ago, accepting my offer of marriage without realizing how the years would trudge. Perhaps she told them of the women's plans, how they would escape the night of the first frost and never return.

I walked between the wheat tillers, squatted, balanced on my haunches and combed the firm white shoots with my fingers. In spring, I would roll the ground. The dark hum of the plow would consolidate the soil around the roots and remedy the snow's disruption to the land. Some things couldn't be negotiated.

I started to search for the women in the woods nearest our house. Each night I pulled on a stocking cap and traversed a new area. I measured my footsteps through the wet leaves, careful not to trip on a fallen tree trunk or a broken root thin as a toddler's arm. I planned to sneak up on them unaware. The women left without notice and I would find them in that same manner. I looked for flashlights, listened to the wind for wisps of giggling, a baby crying. Surely they'd leave some hint. I imagined Marlene being cajoled into the plan by the other women, but as they herded together, Marlene was dropping bits of lint or pieces of her long graying hair for me to find.

Some days I woke in our bed sweaty, the sun a pale apricot, my head aching. I saw Marlene tied to a tree, flames licking at her ankles, screaming my name. And what could I do but tell her I'd find her, that she'd be okay. Perhaps it was a contest Marlene had entered for a million dollars, and she was off, fighting against the other women for the prize, and as soon as she conquered the competition, she'd return, arms outstretched toward me.

None of the men in Mokena discussed what happened. It was embarrassing to talk about the women. We didn't know where they went, what they were doing. There were small underground groups that formed, searched for the women. Some dressed in black and brandished sharp blades and bars of chocolate. One group met for prayers at the town hall underneath the solemn green faces of the Vietnam Veterans Memorial. At the hardware store I learned of a small group of elderly men who found success with boxes of perishables they left evenings at the foot of the forest—apples and cashmere sweaters, toys for the children and glass cut bottles of French perfume; by dawn these boxes would be gone.

Late one night, a few miles from this drop-off point, I was searching for the women when I heard a whispered silence, unlike the sound of bare sugar maples and white-lobed paper birches. I felt something strong rippling in the pricked air. I followed the feeling. I walked for hours. My cheeks flushed and I quickened my steps. I put my hands out in front of me and tucked myself in back of the tall bodies of trees. Suddenly the woods opened up to a clearing. There were fires blazing and two women standing guard in front of one of them, warming their hands. I hid behind a white oak. I recognized both of the women. One worked for the post office and the other was a veterinarian who once delivered a calf for us. She was Marlene's age and seeing the soft rings around her eyes made me well up inside.

I rubbed at my nose and moved forward. Tents surrounded the two blazes in an awkward semi-circle. I noticed the cardboard box of provisions set just outside the fire ring.

Hi David, said the vet. She spoke my name clearly, as if it was no surprise finding me in the country of women when they'd been gone over a month.

Evening, I said to them both. The postal carrier looked suspiciously at me and I pulled my hands out of my pockets, let them drop to my sides. I wanted them to see I didn't mean any harm.

Pretty nippy, huh? asked the vet.

I nodded and held my hands above the flames. I asked,

Marlene around?

The tents were the old army type, camouflage green canvas. The postal worker grimaced and stepped away, slid into one of the tents. I hadn't thought of a realistic plan of rescue. I had expected hostility and seething anger, not cordialness and easy acquiescence. Marlene strode out of the tent a few minutes later and the vet excused herself. Marlene's hair was rolled up on the top of her head like the mornings I found her in the barn, bent over the cows. The fire flickered in her eyes. She looked peaceful and warm and I wanted nothing more than to wrap her up inside my coat and take her home, snuggle with her in our old bed, stiff with years.

She put her arms around me. My eyes became wet.

Sshhh. It's all right, she said, smoothing my thinning hair. I kissed her face all over and she took my hand, led me to a longer tent farthest from the fires. She smiled so sweetly; I put one finger up to her mouth, just to touch those lips. Inside the tent were rows of cots and sleeping bags. I saw Jerry Chimera and his wife nestled together, our neighbors—even the pastor of our church and his wife. Marlene walked over to an empty cot. So many questions came to mind, but when she pulled me down onto the cot I lost sight of where I was. I forgot about all the other married couples from Mokena lined up beside us. She covered our shoulders with a blanket and lifted up her nightgown, and I unbuckled my pants.

When I woke, I was the only person in the tent and the morning sun warmed the canvas to a bright yellow-green. I dressed quickly and peeked outside. One group of women surrounded a fire where some thick red soup boiled in a pot. The sound of children's high squeals filled the air while another group of women sat in a circle, waving their hands. Before I'd taken two steps, Marlene was at my side. She looped her arm inside mine and we started walking toward the long, straight trunks of trees.

Good, good, I instructed. Now once we get to the edge, we're going to start running.

Marlene stopped. Oh dear, she said. I've confused you. I'm not going anywhere. She unlinked her arm from mine and pressed my hand. Her skin felt smooth and soft. You can visit, she said. Like the rest of the men. Whenever you'd like, but not more than twice a week.

I took in air sharply, took the knit cap out of my pocket and pulled it over my ears.

Take care, she called out, her words hitting my neck and back.

*I* only went back to see Marlene one other time. In town, we never talked about the women, but we saw each other in the tent, when the sky turned black and hid our faces. Plans of rescue drafted when I first discovered her whereabouts were pushed aside. My questions went unanswered. What had we done wrong? Why couldn't we arrive at some agreement with the women? Why didn't they return to Mokena for short visits like when we came to see them? I still don't know what I did wrong.

# *Wife Swapping with a Giant*

*B*elieve me when I say it isn't easy to swap wives. You don't forget your first wife as quickly as you might think, especially when you've been married seventeen years, like Donna and me. I'd become accustomed to certain things, like leaning over to kiss her, her eyes blinking up at me. Now, every time I look out the kitchen window the belly of my new wife obstructs my view and I am reminded how things have changed.

The thing to remember is there's no going back. I can't go back on my word, especially not to a giant. This one's name is Gilloph. He is my next-door neighbor and now he lives with my previous wife and no matter what, I've got to try to look okay with this situation. I can't let him think I'm dissatisfied with his wife nor can I let him know the truth: I never thought I could be so content. I have to disguise my feelings either way.

We define ourselves through our struggles. My problem has always been with the truth. I tiptoe around it, deny it, conceal it, and assume others will see right through my lies. The first time I realized my problem I was around ten years old and I'd told my friend Todd that my little sister had x-ray vision. My sister and I were in Todd's basement and I was supposed to be watching her. Todd and I were fooling with his Matchbox cars and he didn't believe me at first. We had made a parking garage with wooden blocks and were speeding down the ramp and crashing into parked cars. Todd had rammed into my red Mustang several times and he was starting to annoy me. So I continued to tell him about my sister's x-ray vision and its potential; the longer he refused to believe, the more elaborate my explanation of her powers became. I told Todd that she could see through walls and doors and caskets—even clothes. I wasn't going anywhere fast, but the notion of naked bodies piqued his interest.

Meanwhile, my six-year-old sister was watching cable and her eyes had glossed over, lips parted just slightly; she wasn't even aware we were talking about her. Todd looked over at her, and then elbowed me. I knew what he was thinking. With my sister's help, he would always know what color underwear the girls in our class were wearing.

I followed Todd to his room where he pulled a crimped twenty-dollar bill from the lacquered box he kept beneath his bed. Once I slipped that bill into the pocket of my Levi's, I sold him my sister for three weeks.

I went home to a dinner of pork chops and told my parents my sister was eating with the neighbors across the street. Half an hour later, we were just finishing our salads when my sister ran into the house crying, clenching her fingers and blubbering even harder when she looked at me.

My parents grounded me for a month and I wasn't allowed to say more than hello to Todd. My father took me out to the garage and boxed my ears that night. "Whatsa matter with you? Are you crazy?" I knew better than to answer any one of his questions, but after he slammed the door of my room, I heard him tell my mother, "The kid's insane!"

She didn't argue with him.

$D$onna and I met after she sideswiped my truck on Sixth Avenue. I was approaching a stoplight and she merged right into the passenger side. My cheeks swelled with air, my face flushed blood red. I was only a few years out of high school while she was finishing her last semester. I'd bought the truck with my own money and she had nearly taken off the passenger door. I walked over to her, measured my breathing, and when I looked down at those brown berry eyes of hers she started crying, reaching for the sleeve of my flannel like it was the most natural thing. Three months later, we had a ceremony in my uncle's backyard.

At the time I didn't question why Donna might marry someone like me. I figured I was lucky. She hung out with the popular crowd who attended football games in a caravan and afterwards, met for pizza at Aurelio's. She was one of the loveliest girls at Milver High School. While I didn't have as much going for me, I was clean-shaven and fiddling with cars for over half my life had sculpted my muscles. I figured I was lucky to marry her, although if I could go back, I'd make myself sit and think about why she might be interested in a guy like me.

Being around Donna, I felt like I had a purpose—that I was worth more than just making a rattle disappear from beneath some guy's car. When she was at my side it was like a proclamation to the world that I was OKAY. It's only the last couple months that I have doubted everything.

With Donna around, suddenly there was someone to listen to my bad days. A lot of men say their wives are their best friends, and really, for a time, Donna was mine.

There comes a time it's just too late to relive a life. The giant's wife and I share a different closeness. I live with a giant now, but I will never forget when Donna and I were just a normal couple.

Maybe our marriage would have turned out differently if we'd had kids. I think Donna might have enjoyed being a mother. I would have liked kids and always wanted them; somewhere along the way a baby became an impossibility. Donna kissed my cheek rather than my lips. During the day she patted my shoulder rather than slipping her hand in the back pocket of my jeans, and she turned away from me in bed. I blamed it on economics—I'd never had steady work and Donna was the type of girl that expected things—shiny, expensive things I couldn't afford. What kind of life would I be able to offer a child? The giant's wife says that I have a heart as big as Lake Erie and that will feed a child more than any paycheck. Maybe if Donna had believed this, things might have turned out otherwise.

*I* remember how Donna and I speculated when the bulldozers started digging next to our property. "Maybe it's some type of car plant," said Donna. We were standing in our bare feet, cupping mugs of coffee. What she said was hopeful. I'd been laid off from the dealership for more than a month, and I knew Donna was doing a little sewing and other odd jobs behind my back. I'd dipped into our savings account to make the house payment and I started accruing bills on our Visa. It wasn't the first time we had to make things stretch.

"Or it could be a sports complex for some major league team," I said.

"Could be." Donna put her hand behind my neck for a moment. Every day we watched the progress: cinder blocks embedded in the foundation, enormous wood beams, layers of pink insulation. Once we saw masons laying bricks, we knew it was something much more extravagant than an industrial complex. And the building's shape and tiered roof did not lend itself to any sports stadium. At some point they finished the brick house, an enormous gaping structure the height of half a city block.

The longer I remained unemployed, the more agitated I became. Donna started staying later in town, her job as a seamstress at Zannie's Fabrics no longer a secret. I crafted eight different resumes. I said I was a chef, a masseuse, even a veterinary assistant. Whatever ad I read in the *Chronicle*, I became. I hadn't played the drums since I was in the eleventh grade, and suddenly I found myself trying out for the Lightning Owls, a local band that played weddings and proms. After the audition they said they'd call and set something up; they never did. Life is sometimes like that, giving you direction when you don't have any. It's obvious I wasn't pursuing the right path. Who knew happiness was right next door?

I started to see myself as potential employers did—too bald, too overweight, too old, and too stupid. And for the first time in our seventeen years together, I started lying to Donna as well. I slept in. I spent the day in my boxers and a sweatshirt. I told Donna I'd found a job tabulating some data from home for an accountant. I even shaved my beard. She never asked who I was working for—we knew most everyone in town. Donna is a smart woman and she knows me better than I know myself. I even considered she might have known I was fibbing. Still, I'd rather believe she was too occupied by her own projects.

I was watching *Hollywood Squares* from my armchair, when Gilloph knocked. At the door, all I could see was a khaki-colored column, like two elm trunks dressed in Dockers. Gilloph's head ended somewhere near the top of a two-story building. I squinted to see his face. "I'm your new neighbor, Gilloph," and he thrust out a hand the size of a rake. My hand rested on top of his thumb.

"Nice to meet you." I tried to keep my voice even-paced and light. One step and he could squash our house.

Gilloph is a talker and with his booming voice people naturally quiet. Standing right there on my lawn he told me he and his wife had both grown up in the Ohio Valley and they were excited to be back. He talked about his hobbies—the stock market, sailing, the breeding of Pomeranian dogs. I didn't know if he meant the regular dogs or if these were giant-sized as well. I stood there knotting and re-knotting the belt of my robe.

"Hey, bud, who does your landscaping?" Gilloph fanned his arm out at our lawn and a few birds squawked.

"I do," I said.

"NO kidding! You're a landscaper. What luck. I need someone to get the grounds of our place in order and keep them that way." I simply nodded my head and, well, things took off from there. Other than employment, I didn't want to have anything to do with the giants. Donna was the one who became friends with the giant's wife and arranged our first dinner. I had already decided not to like them. At some point I forgot this resolution.

*T*he first time Donna and I were invited to the giants' house, we both fell into a shy stupor. The interior was as spectacular as the exterior. There were the usual things you'd expect in a giant's house—seemingly endless ceilings, a winding staircase with steep steps—a red sofa the size of a school bus and a painting on the wall nearly matched its dimensions.

Donna marveled at our good fortune; she mentioned how difficult it was to make friends at our age. Suddenly there were dinners at the giants' house and games of bocce. Since the giant's wife was a quarter Italian, she served us veal scaloppini, grilled portabella mushrooms, and asti spumante wine. Gilloph tenderly picked up Donna and sat her in one of the high chairs they brought out when we visited. When I saw her trim waist nestled between Gilloph's hands, I thought nothing of it. He picked me up with the same gentleness.

Gilloph and his wife also had areas of the house that were distinctly theirs. His wife collected antique books and human-sized games like Life and Monopoly. She treated them like knick knacks that nearly disappeared in the palm of her hand. They decorated the room off the TV area, which I would have called the study, but Gilloph referred to as the joy room.

Every time Donna and I ate dinner at the giants' house, we'd usually convene to the joy room for coffee and port, maybe a cigar for Gilloph and me. The giant's wife wasn't the only one that kept special objects in the joy room. Gilloph himself had a train set, each car the size of our microwave. The train glistened and smelled newly oiled. While we were talking about politics or the local zoning of our town, I'd wander over to the train and stare at its land. There was a hill that separated the town while the downtown was comprised of a series of older two-story storefronts. A wide-loaded courthouse created the town square with pine trees on every corner and white lights strung between light posts. I'd notice something different in the set each time we entered the joy room. For instance, the elementary and high schools were named Gordon and Milver, the names of our town founders, just like the schools in Highland. The parking lot of the supermarket had a covered cart return just like the one at our grocery store.

The third or fourth time they had us over for dinner, we were in the joy room and Gilloph heard me chuckling. He leaned over toward me. "What's the joke, bud?"

"Some of this looks like Highland."

"What does?" His voice starched.

I pointed out the names of the streets and he pulled out an elaborate gold-chromed magnifying glass. He peered at the street signs through the square of glass. "Is there a section of our town with those street names?" he asked. "I fashioned them from the German town where my family originated."

"Well you can drive down those very streets in Highland."

"No kidding," he said. "That's a coincidence."

And then he took out an enormous bottle of wine. He rested his tongue on his top lip and concentrated on filling my human-sized glass.

The next morning when I told Donna that Gilloph was creating a diorama of our town, she showed a good deal of surprise. "Maybe it's like a giant's version of a map—it's his way of understanding where everything is located." We were eating scrambled eggs and we had plans to visit the zoo that day. Gilloph had given me the morning off and as a surprise, I had planned to pick up a picnic lunch from one of Donna's favorite restaurants, Chez Lou, and drive her to the lake.

Donna seemed pleased that suddenly I wasn't stuck beneath some greasy car. After spending some time outdoors, my face tanned and while my hands were still filthy, it was easier to wash off dirt than try to dig grease from beneath my fingernails. Obviously Donna knew I'd stretched the truth a bit when I accepted the job offer from Gilloph, but I could take care of some shrubs, get rid of crabgrass, plant some flowers, a tree or two. The grounds were easily as large as a football field and covered with sod I helped plant. With my new job, I had restored Donna's faith in me, and without her saying a thing, I again felt righted. Just being around Donna made you feel like you were something out of the ordinary. I suppose that's why Gilloph was interested in her as well, only he was a giant and who thought that giants were attracted to the rest of us normal-sized people?

For weeks after Gilloph and his wife first moved in, people from Highland and nearby towns drove by in their cars in hopes of seeing them. Once the giants became Donna's friends, she'd mention their names in casual conversation to our average-sized acquaintances. For instance, we'd be buying groceries and people would asked us, "What do they talk about?"

Donna would explain, "They're normal people, they just happen to be larger than most folks."

Then they'd ask, "Have they ever eaten humans?" This angered Donna, her chest heaving, rumbling in a way I'd never before witnessed.

"Do you eat humans?" she'd ask right back. Her sudden viciousness would surprise locals and just as quickly, Donna would return to her good-natured self. "Why don't you stop by their house some time and say hello? I'm sure the giants would love to meet you."

"Well sure," they'd reply, eager to end the conversation. "That sounds great." They never would visit, of course. Gradually, people became accustomed to the giants' residency and the line of cars snaking past their house disappeared.

I didn't say much during these exchanges. While I'd grown familiar with the giants, I didn't feel the same sense of pride in our friendship as Donna.

*D*onna and the giant's wife spent a good deal of time together. They exchanged recipes. Donna super-sized her favorite dishes while the giant's wife used a complicated equation to reduce hers. They enjoyed online shopping at the same stores, although the giant's wife still purchased her clothes from a tailor in

Germany. Donna seemed happier. She was still doing some sewing on the side, but it was definitely an afterthought. I was working again and Gilloph was paying me well. Sometimes the giant's wife would invite Donna over for lunch and while I was making the evergreens into topiaries of butterflies and birds, I'd hear them laughing. Donna had been voted one of the most popular girls at Milver High School and she was beginning to act as carefree as when I'd first met her.

"Don't you think it seems odd to create a model of the town where you live?" I asked Donna one evening as we readied to go to the giants' house.

"Who's to say what's odd for giants," countered Donna. It was weird. The whole thing was odd from the start. Why did they choose Highland? Why did they want to live next door to us? Why did they want to be our friends? Not all of these questions remained unanswered.

It was Wednesday and we had gotten into the habit of playing pinochle with the giants and eating blue cheeseburgers, which Donna told me was an expensive cheese. Sometimes we played Scrabble on a special-made board. We separated into teams and it was Donna's idea to mix things up. Donna and Gilloph were one team, the giant's wife and I became another. I've never been much of a reader, so it was no surprise when Donna and Gilloph won. Donna put down 'recidivism' and Gilloph applauded, which sounded like fireworks. What was more shocking was how they carried on during the game. Gilloph leaned in real close when Donna showed him her words, or Donna tapped his chin when Gilloph tried to prick her with his beard.

The giant's wife and I just smiled at each other and said encouraging things when we placed a word down. The way Donna and Gilloph were carrying on was embarrassing. If the situation had been reversed and I was flirting with the giant's wife, I'd like to think Donna or Gilloph would have been equally upset. So instead of saying anything, I kept accepting the imported beers Gilloph handed me. When the giant's wife yawned, I was pleased to say good night. Donna and I walked the forty some feet to our house; I was nearly drunk and very angry. I couldn't find the keyhole for the lock and banged on the door with my fist.

"Tom! Let me." Donna opened the door quietly but I felt anything but calm. I ripped off my shoes and threw them against the ceiling. I pulled off the button-down shirt Donna had made me wear and flung it into the air.

"How about *carnage* or *infidelity*?" I yelled. "Where were those bonus words?"

Donna stood against the door still holding the keys in her fist.

I turned to her, walked in close. "Don't take me for stupid." I stumbled upstairs and fell asleep on top of the comforter, still wearing my pants. The next day I woke crumpled on her side of the bed and realized I'd spent the night alone.

About this time I started making jokes about Gilloph. We had a giant living next door to us, one of the most rare individual forms, maybe fifteen or twenty living in the entire world and I wasn't taking full advantage of the comic potential. Just innocent stuff, like one afternoon I returned from working at Gilloph's and found Donna reading a hardcover book on the couch.

"How'd it go?" she asked.

"Fine, but don't head out there without a gas mask. Gilloph had burritos for lunch."

"I don't think that's necessary, Tom." Now she was the serious one.

The next time we were at Gilloph's house for dinner, even

more had been added to the model of our town. There were different colored flags at the Chevy dealership where I used to work. A family of four biked along the trail at Briar Woods. And then I noticed our house—Donna's and mine—next to the giants' sprawling estate. There was a small balding man in dark pants with clippers in his hands working on the rose bushes that outlined the giants' property. I was a little surprised that Gilloph had placed me at his house rather than my own, but that feeling was quickly replaced by anger once I glanced at the backyard of Gilloph's estate and saw Donna. There was an enormous pool the size of a parking lot at the back of the house. Gilloph and his wife didn't have a swimming pool, but that didn't throw me off in any way. Donna was stretched out in a chaise lounge wearing a red bikini. Sitting beside her was another man—the giant—only reduced to the size of a Barbie. He had a trim beard and a short-sleeved shirt stretched taut across his chest. He was smoothing lotion onto her arms and she was looking at him like he was the greatest thing that ever walked the earth.

I paused for a second, waited until I heard them talking. They were discussing the controversial housing development planned near the protected wetlands.

"They're birds!" said Gilloph, "They can fly elsewhere!"

His wife disagreed and Donna kept saying, "It's a difficult issue all the way around."

I moved the doll of Donna. I took her scantily-clad body and hid her behind the shed by the model of our house. I remained clipping the bushes.

"How's it going over there?" asked Gilloph, wandering over near me. The last thing I'd heard Gilloph booming about was what he'd do if he was elected mayor.

"Just noticed the pool here at your house."

"I don't have a pool, bud. Although funny you should mention it; lately, I've been thinking that'd be a nice addition to the grounds. We've got the land, why not use it?" He chuckled and reached over and slapped my back with two fingers. "Maybe you'll have to start paying me for offering you such a great job!" I grinned thinly.

Later that night, when we were readying for bed, I told Donna about the pool and she laughed. "It's a joke, Tom. Really. Everyone has hobbies and this is Gilloph's."

"Do you own a bikini?" I asked.

Donna sighed. "You've seen my underwear many times."

"A bathing suit," I said. "A red one. "

"Well, at one time, yes. Years ago."

$I$ woke up the next day well rested and determined not to let Gilloph push me around. I went to his place and fiddled in his garage with a new anti-weed spray. It would take most of the morning to spray the lawn and I wanted to start early. Gilloph came outside in his robe, munching on a loaf of bread.

"Starting early today," he announced.

"You know what they say."

"Sure do," said Gilloph, crumbs tumbling out of his mouth and onto the lawn. "Well, I'm going to be out for a few hours and I think the wives have something planned, as well."

"Manicures," I said.

"Help yourself to a Coke when you'd like one."

"Will do!" I waved him off with the hose. I waited for about an hour after Gilloph's wife had left with Donna and the sun strode high in the sky; it was just the giant's house, me, and the model of Highland. I took my shoes off at the door and carefully made my way to the study. Everything seemed even larger without the giant or his wife looming nearby. Luckily the door to the study was open, as the handle was well over my head and I didn't have the patience to figure out how to open it.

I walked over to the model and found the doll of Donna back in her place next to the pool. I grabbed her and shoved her in my shirt pocket. I hoped Gilloph wouldn't miss the doll and even if he did, I didn't care. Donna was mine.

I sprayed the front lawn and took a Coke out of the refrigerator in the garage. I sipped my drink beneath a maple sapling and patted the doll in my pocket, the arches of her feet curling over the edge of my shirt. The doll had Donna's brown eyes and a mole on the neck under her left ear. I felt like it was New Year's Eve and I was making resolutions to change my present course. There was a distance growing between Donna and me that I didn't like. Donna meant the world to me eighty times over and I thought that was apparent.

I finished the back lawn and then returned home where I hid the doll in the back of my sock drawer. I took the newspaper onto the back patio, opened up a lawn chair in the sun, and ended up dozing. When I woke, the sky had clouded over a full gray. Donna was inside stuffing a chicken and her cheeks were flushed. She was wearing a gold bracelet I didn't recognize and it slid up and down her arm as she moved. She told me Gilloph had stopped over and wanted to speak with me.

"I'll go over for a minute," I told her. "I'll be back for dinner." Donna wanted to see the new Travolta film and it was showing at seven o'clock at the cineplex.

Gilloph was in the game room playing pool on a billiards table the size of a racquetball court. I enjoyed playing the game myself but had never done so with Gilloph because of the awkward size of his table. "Up for a game?" he asked, his gaze unwavering. As a result of the day's events, I was feeling particularly ingenious, so I agreed.

"I played pro tourneys for a bit in the late eighties," I told him.

"You don't say!"

"You sure you're up for losing?" I said. "I'd hate to spoil your night."

"You won't spoil my night," said Gilloph. "No way."

I pushed the fib further. "I was really good. Guys used to call me 'Sure Shot.'"

"Well, then I'm really looking forward to this," said Gilloph. He handed me a stick for a normal-sized human. There was an extension ladder leaning against the bookcase that I used to make my shots. Gilloph insisted I go first: solids. I sunk two off the back wall. He sunk all six of his balls within two turns. I couldn't just give him that. In the next game I called up every reserve I had from years of Wednesday night bowling with the guys from the dealership. I imagined myself in a slick red shirt, the soft kind that opened in an extra-wide V. I saw a spotlight overhead; all normal-sized men trying to make an honest living cheered me on. I was cleaning up, three more solids to go, when Gilloph started talking.

"What a lucky man you are. Donna's such a beautiful woman." If he was trying to jolt my focus he was badly mistaken. My veins constricted—my blood ran thin. I became a machine, an eight-ball king! He might be a giant with an amazing house and more money than I would ever have, but I had the real prize.

I sank three more, one into the corner pocket. It was his shot and he had only two balls left. "How about a small wager?" asked Gilloph.

Finally I saw Gilloph for the monster he was. He wasn't some gentle, well-meaning neighbor, as Donna would describe him; he was a jerk, a pompous fool, with his fancy furniture and lush topiaries that *I* designed. I might have seemed stupid, with my full hand of bravado, to even consider his offer. Why couldn't I have said no, that Donna meant too much to me to bet on her? Yet I played exactly because she *did* mean so much to me. "You're on," I said.

"Winner gets a date with your wife," he said.

"If I win, what do I get?"

"I'll give you five hundred dollars and you and Donna can spend it as you please."

Even though I'd reaffirmed myself to Donna, the notion of winning that kind of money and spending it freely was tempting. Didn't both Donna and I deserve some of the accumulated wealth of these two giants? Hadn't we worked just as hard? I could easily say I was tricked, and perhaps I was, but truly, when I leaned over from the top rung of the ladder and reached up for Gilloph's hairy hand, I believed he would miss his final shots and I would win.

*T*he night before Donna's date with Gilloph, we turned in to bed early. The moon waxed and the light shone through the flimsy curtains. I could hear Donna breathing, could feel the weight of her chest rising and falling, although not a finger touched her and it was only the feather comforter over us that we shared. "I'm sorry," is what I meant to say a thousand times—it leapt out of every centimeter of my body. I was certain she was angry and upset about the whole thing. I leaned over and kissed her forehead—the one place that was smooth and arched and looked just as perfect as the day we met on Sixth Avenue. Donna remained motionless—just the sound of her breathing, and I returned to my side of the bed.

"Tom." Donna rolled over and put her arms around me. She

held me in a way that eased me; a hug that told me things would be just fine.

When I woke the next morning, she was already gone. Gilloph was taking her sailing for most of the day and his own wife, quite matter-of-fact about the whole thing, had invited me over for lunch. I pulled some weeds around the begonias and raked the dirt along the edge of the shed in our backyard. Afterward, I went home, freshened up, and walked over to Gilloph's house in a clean white shirt.

The giant's wife served shrimp scampi on the porch and re-filled my glass with fresh-squeezed lemonade. She was wearing a loose sweater that plunged low. When she handed me the bread-basket, my eyes accidentally caught on the line of cleavage streak-ing from her top and I quickly looked away. Surprisingly, I felt myself blush and tighten with excitement, something I hadn't felt in years.

She ate three plates of the tiny curled shellfish and talked about her sisters who lived in Germany. When she spoke I heard the soft twist of her native tongue. The giant's wife and I had a polite conversation and then I excused myself and returned home, fell asleep in front of the TV.

Donna didn't come home that night after her date with Gilloph, or even the next. Was I supposed to break down doors for her? I did so inconspicuously, visiting Gilloph's home and ask-ing his wife's opinion for some tulip bulbs I wanted to plant the following spring. My conversations with his wife were nothing stel-lar, but they were ringed with comfort and I found my eyes resting on the soft roundness of her bottom.

A few days after Donna had left for her date, I saw her sitting on Gilloph's shoulder wearing a halter dress and hoop earrings. She looked fantastic. The giant's wife knocked at my door crying and blubbering and the tears nearly washed out the impatiens and red dahlias growing beneath the front picture window. Gilloph had told his own wife to leave; he barely gave her the chance to pack a suitcase. I gave her a roll of toilet paper and made her some tea and the two of us sat outside under the stars and watched the flickering lights at Gilloph's house. We heard laughter and glasses clinking and no matter what, I was prepared to forgive Donna. Certainly she'd return within a few days.

It's not the first time I've been wrong.

What I've learned about living with a giant is nothing you could read in a textbook. The giant's wife plays the radio and hums along to light rock. She doesn't believe in saving leftovers and demands that I clean my plate. I've become accustomed to the concern she shows for my health. I've started taking a multivitamin and in the mornings, I do forty sit-ups before breakfast. The giant's wife encourages me, as well. When she saw me carrying around the community college course catalogue, she told me to get on the phone and register that minute. And you know what? I listened to her. The first time I left for class, I felt unbelievably happy. She waved as I drove off with my new notebooks and pens. Maybe there's something in giants that allows them to look into the future and see all possibilities rather than one narrow stretch of highway, the way the normal-sized seem to view things.

Although I think about Donna, I don't let myself dwell on all our years together. And even though I am learning a good deal in my psychology class, what good would it do to begin analyzing our time together? I know my intentions were misguided.

There are things the giant's wife and I share that I never could with Donna. We've gone to Cincinnati for baseball games and instead of buying tickets, the giant's wife will place me on her shoulders and we'll watch the game outside the park. We share chores around the house. The giant's wife and I clean the gutters together—she picks me up and I dig out the debris. I am also helpful to the giant's wife. Twice a month, I take my tweezers and she holds me close to her face while I help trim her eyebrows. We divide up responsibilities and no task is left to just one of us. Both of us have found this lifestyle suits us quite well.

We've hired a contractor to remodel the house and he's planning to eliminate the second floor, creating a ceiling over nineteen feet. In the meanwhile, I sleep outside with the giant's wife. Here's the funny thing: although the giant's wife and I don't have that much in common, when she moves her hands along my back, my toes curl. She feels more right than anyone ever has. When we kiss my lips fit in the middle of hers and our tongues touch, mine running along the edge of hers, her tongue covering mine. I hear the giant's wife loud and clear at night beneath the stars. She reaches toward me and I lean toward her, our bodies speaking words our healing hearts cannot.

# The Strongest Woman in the World

Muscles are comprised of striated muscle fibers. They expand with use. Mine are as hard as the heads of babies; they cut my shoulders and outline the sleeves of my sweater even though it's long-sleeved and loose and I've chosen it specifically to disguise the brawn of my figure. Tonight, I'd like to conceal the fact that I am the strongest woman in the world.

I just might be the last single woman, as well; at least, that's how my married friends talk. They've known me since grade school when they were the only ones who weren't afraid of me—they had their own problems. One of my friends has two different-sized legs. Her left leg is three times the girth of the right and she has to specially tailor her pants. My other friend has skin decorated with fist-sized blisters. With age they've both found ways to compensate for their awkwardness. I have only recently begun to suppress my strength.

My friends always comfort my depressed moods with well-meaning advice. They encourage me to wear more makeup and skirts, stuff my bra, and wear three-inch heels even though it will push my height beyond six feet. "Heels provide the illusion of trim legs," my sister reminds me over the phone, an hour before this evening's blind date. She has called four times to remind me to cross my legs when I'm seated and to wear my hair up. "It's too short to stay up," I told her.

"Then use hairspray," she demands.

"It's still going to fall."

She sighed a long breath and it sounded as though she was exhaling a cigarette. But she's six months pregnant with her third child and I know her days of smoking and boozing have long since passed. Mine have not. I frequent local watering holes in hopes of increasing my chances of meeting a man. Truthfully, no amount of beer has secured me a boyfriend. That was how this evening came to be.

My sister and I finally compromise on my hairstyle and now plastic combs hold the sides back. "You want him to be attracted to you, not fear you." Only my sister doesn't understand what it's like to be as speedy as eighty horses, to have the power of a Mack truck, and simultaneously wear a size-A cup.

My sister is a mother, courteous and kind. She doesn't curse or wear her jeans more than a day without washing them. I don't know why she isn't equally as strong as I am. Our parents were ordinary people. They grew up outside of Chicago twenty miles from each other, a fifteen-minute drive on Interstate 94. Their cells divided and differentiated into muscle cells just like those of normal humans. I used to hold my mother responsible for my strength. "It's your gift from God," she told me every time I returned from elementary school crying, because my classmates refused to let me play kickball. No matter how I tried, every time it was my turn I kicked the ball miles out of town and it invariably shot through the front window of some elderly man's home. Instead, my classmates forced me to serve as referee and hung a whistle around my neck.

Believe me when I say I am past the point of blame.

I used to enjoy being the strongest woman, like when I was called to San Jose, California, to hold a bridge steady after an especially violent earthquake. I hung beneath the bridge and held two split slabs together, the twisted cables secure beneath my hands, while the cars overhead traveled on their way. But I am tired of saving other people. There is no pleasure in being strong on nights like tonight when I slip into the dating pool and it is as if I only know a feeble, gaspy sidestroke. And this one, according to my sister, is my type. She hasn't stopped talking about this blind date since she first brought it up a few weeks ago. "You're going to be crazy about Gerald—he runs and drinks those powdered drinks they sell at the health food store." I think it's funny my sister thinks she knows my type. I always considered myself like that Greek legend Sisyphus, condemned to push a huge boulder to the top of a mountain only to have it roll down the other side. An endless task. Only I am cursed with strength. I don't need to lift weights. My muscles generate on their own. They dip into my shoulders and sculpt my forearms and back. This is not the result of any bottled drink.

Last night I spoke with Gerald on the phone. He was quiet and I found myself doing the greater part of the talking. I asked him about his work, his family, how he knows my sister. The only thing he asked me is where I wanted to meet him. When I discovered he lives in Wilmette, I knew it was pointless. I have a slim chance with the city guys while the ones from the north suburbs are a lost cause. They have too many manicured women from which to choose.

Still, I agreed to meet him at a bar in Lakeview, Ginger's Tap, halfway between both our homes. I told him I'd be wearing a red sweater, that I was tall and fit with brown hair. I did not tell him I could bench him and his apartment building, if he so desired. Since an average woman would have to drive the ten miles, I take a bus. I'd much rather prefer to run the distance, although ruining my mascara would anger my sister. Sometimes she shows up unexpectedly during these social events to approve my clothes and makeup. I realize she is trying to be helpful. Yet no matter how hard I smile when she approaches during the middle of a date, my eyes well up and I must pretend it's allergies.

Her presence is a continual reminder that I am the one to pity.

Tonight, I am wearing heels, so I take tiny steps from the bus stop to the entrance of Ginger's Tap. The bar is a deep redwood color swaddled in layers of polyurethane. I take a seat facing the door, order a vodka tonic and look around. It's not glamorous, but tiny candles flicker in glass jars on round tables giving the room a jack-o-lantern feeling. Two felt-worn pool tables are set near the back by the restrooms and right now two overweight men in bib overalls are vying for the table with two young lawyer-types. I have my money on the men wearing the bibs. I am the only woman here, but it doesn't bother me. At work I am the only woman as well. I scale over the city in a hard hat, welding vertical members and beams, blue sparks flying past my goggles. I affix metal sheets to withstand wind stress and the straps of my harness whip about. When I applied to work the high girders, they put me through every physical test imaginable. They timed how quickly I could embed steel columns in a concrete foundation, a stopwatch fast at my side. They counted the number of pull-ups I could do in a minute. Initially their tests didn't bother me. I liked proving I could do the work.

I was twenty-two before I ventured beyond my parents' home and learned how to manage my muscle. At that time I didn't use my strength to help just anyone. I received a letter from a boy pleading for me to save the S.S. Edmund Fitzgerald from its watery grave in Lake Superior. The boy and his family wanted me to pull the sunken ship to shore so that they could put his grandfather's remains to rest. At the end of his note he mentioned that when he grew up he wanted to be the strongest man. I couldn't help but oblige. Who doesn't want to be a hero?

It didn't take more than twenty minutes to peel off my corduroys, dive into Lake Superior, and swim out to the ship's wasted scraps. I lifted the bloated stern and held it over my head, kicked off the bottom and dragged part of the ship to shore. It only took three more trips to the submerged bulk carrier before it was on land, reunited with the only other rescued relic, a polished bronze bell. They put my name in the *Guinness Book of World Records* for that save, but to be honest, my name would be listed many more times if I let them. Now I only give fake names when I pry open doors after car accidents, or when NASA asks for my services to return satellite wreckage from the sea.

The Chicago paramedics gave me a beeper and I have my own room with a waterbed at the local fire department. It's not unusual for either of them to page me once a day. But I am tired of being on call. Recently, I have found myself leaving the pager on top of my dresser. I imagine it buzzing for hours, the paramedics waiting for my call, forced to field emergencies with their own mortal skills.

Lately, I crave regular things. I wonder what it would be like to have a spouse. I have found that men do not like women stronger than they are. They want to hold open doors for their partners and beat up ex-boyfriends. They want to hold their girlfriends when they sob during movies staring Richard Gere. The truth is, I never cry at movies. I cry at night when it's just me and my German shepherd mix, Beans, curled on top of our bed and the wind howls and there is only a hairy, forty-five pound dog warm against my legs.

Sometimes I think about marriage. My ideal mate wouldn't mind if I wore tank tops or that my muscles were wider, firmer than any he could produce through repetitions in a gym. He would find my snoring endearing, my nostrils wide and flapping, a herd of antelope ambushing the countryside. Lately, I've been thinking of giving it all up. Someday nature will take my strength from me and I have found heartache pains less viciously when it's chosen. At first it will hurt to be ordinary, although like anything else, I'll grow accustomed to being an average woman. And surely then, I'll find a man. I'll make pancakes on Saturday mornings and plant a garden. I'll ask my husband to lift heavy seedling trays and the watering can. When he rolls over in the middle of the night and reaches for me, I'll wait for him on my back, patient.

After I finish my drink the bartender brings me another one. He smiles at me and I think it must be the makeup, the red sweater. My sister was the one who told me that if a woman wore red it meant she was ready for love. I wish I'd known this sooner. I wear jeans and T-shirts to work. My co-workers don't mind seeing me curl thousand-pound beams of steel or scale hundred-story buildings with my hands. Sometimes they set wagers. They bet I couldn't beat the elevator that runs along the steel skeleton of our latest project. A bunch of them piled in the elevator and cheered me on while I climbed alongside the wobbly cage. I won. They patted my back and told me I'm amazing. Somehow it doesn't feel that way.

The guys from work never invite me out with them for drinks or burgers. The one time I was invited out, one of the supervisors was getting married and when I arrived at the bar, a place called the Honey Pot, there was a disco ball and a revolving stage with dancers, and I was the only woman in attendance dressed in more than a g-string. When I approached their tables the whole lot of them erupted in laughter. "She really came!" howled the new hire. The groom-to-be pushed back his chair in slow motion, eased onto his feet, and sauntered up to me. He slid a creaseless dollar bill into the waistband of my jeans. It was as if my feet sprouted roots. I couldn't move. After what seemed like an eternity, I fled for the exit and never looked back.

My sister thinks I should take an indoor job. She is certain once I am doing something more womanly I will meet a man and there will be no stopping us. While I appreciate her optimism, it's easy for her to say. She is married, bakes good brownies, and is mother to two tow-headed boys who make fart sounds with their armpits. In her world, everything has an explanation.

While waiting for my blind date, I keep my eye on the door of Ginger's Tap, and try to twist the ends of my hair. I smile with my lips closed even though the only thoughts in my head are of false expectations and dashed hopes. My last date was Dale, the brother-in-law of a co-worker I respected. He had sworn he would not tell Dale about my strength. This date and I had agreed to go bowling at Fairview Lanes and during the first game I scored a three hundred without trying. When Dale accused me of practicing, I denied it. He stormed away to call my co-worker from the pay phone. When he returned to our lane, Dale's shirtsleeves were rolled up, his face flushed red. "Let's arm wrestle," he said. When I shook my head, he asked, "Are you chicken? Huh?" I could have flattened his head like a tortilla, bashed in his eyes with my pinky finger, swung his body to Texas. Instead I pushed past him, headed for the exit. "Ain't nothing but a chicken—bawk-bawk," he yelled.

Maybe he's right. Even Dale has an idea of who I am supposed to be.

I am only in my thirties, but age has begun to thread its way into my bones. I know one day I'll wake with arthritis quaking my hands, spurting in my legs. Brown spots dotting my face and neck. I feel myself growing weak. Some nights I dream I shrink and my hands and legs whittle down to the proportions of an average five-feet tall woman. My hair grows long, straight down my back. Suddenly I am able to purchase fashions from the department store and no longer have to order special shoes from catalogues, yet I cannot stop standing on my tiptoes, trying to see beyond the periphery, like those Midwesterners who move to Colorado and become depressed because they cannot see what's on the other side of the Rockies. During those nights I always wake screaming and Beans starts whimpering, his wet nose nudging my elbow.

Inside Ginger's Tap the two-bibbed men high-five one another and one of the lawyers grimaces, begrudgingly buys drinks for the winner. They refill their pints and the bibbed men whoop and holler, lifting their glasses in a rambunctious toast, foam running down their bare arms. The lawyers are quieter; they keep their eyes down and challenge the bibbed men to another game, their voices crisply ironed.

My date has changed his mind, I am nearly certain, when the heavy door needles open. Gerald wags a thick hand at my sweater and lopes toward me, pulling out the stool at my left. He's a good four inches shorter than I am but he's bulky. He orders a beer. "Have you been here long?" he asks. I smile my practiced smile and evade his question, excuse myself. I head to the restroom, as my sister instructed so I appear mysterious and intrigue will outweigh his fear of my size. I touch his sleeve gently as I step away, noting the firmness beneath his shirt. Gerald's protein shakes must be working.

In the bathroom, I look in the mirror. Plain brown eyes, a small nose. I make a muscle and grimace, my world-wrestling face, then dig into the purse on loan from my sister and search for lipstick.

It's easier to pretend to be someone else for a stranger. If I am going to transform myself into an average woman, there are memories I must put away and forget.

Like the time my mother and sister talked me into competing as a man in a wrestling match. It was a year after high school and I was uncertain what to do next with my life. My mother had lost her job and money was tight. My sister brought home a brochure for a wrestling match advertising a fifty-thousand-dollar prize.

They dressed me in shimmery electric-colored shorts, a stretchy tank top that flattened my nearly non-existent breasts and they cut my hair even shorter than it is now. My wrestling name was Titan and I only enrolled for the prize money.

The amateur match was nothing like the costumes and song and dance on TV. It took less than two minutes for me to beat my opponent and then another to go on to wrestle the defending champ, Zephyr the Great. When Zephyr entered the ring they played a special song and a single spotlight shone on his bald head; the crowd erupted into cheers when he held his gold prize belt in the air. For a moment, I was excited to step into the ring in my shiny outfit—maybe they'd cheer for me as well. With a single match I could become a wrestling champ and they would refer to me as Titan the Great.

With the bell signal, Zephyr and I circled one another in the boxing ring. His oiled skin glistened. I dove in and tackled his legs and lifted him over my shoulder. I was surprised by how light he felt in my hands. I began to spin him slowly, imagining the audience's ecstatic cheers. I spun him faster, air cupping under my armpits, my own head swirling. That's when my fingers slipped and Zephyr fell from my hands. His head slammed into the mat, a heavy dull sound. His tiny eyes rolled back into his head. Someone pushed me off into the corner. Zephyr's mother and fiancé sped into the ring, their tears falling on his chest's tightly wound curls. I waited for his head to pop up, a grimace painting his face. The audience stood dumfounded. He did not wake up. I was certain it was some joke until three security guards in black silk-screened jackets cloaked my sides and escorted me to the locker room.

I did not become their hero. I put my head down and did not lift it for three years until I traveled to Michigan and pulled the S.S. Fitzgerald to shore.

Much to my sister and mother's chagrin, I gave the prize money away to charity. I took a job stocking shelves during the midnight shift at Cub Foods. Gradually, I put my head back together. I moved out of my mother's suburbs and into the city. I rented my own apartment and began using my power to resolve tragedies rather than cause them.

Time has passed and I hear many clocks inside me ticking. My sister believes women in their thirties emit baby-producing hormones. A man can sniff out fertility and take her home, bed her down easier than other women. I am not sure if I want kids. I am certain it will hurt and no strength in the world will suppress the body being ripped and torn, another creature flooding out, gulping for air, its mouth a black pit. What if I pass this strength on to my children? My sons would become NFL players no doubt, but what about my daughters? What sort of life is there for women strong enough to halt avalanches? If I had a daughter, I would send her to my sister's for long visits and together we would teach her how to disguise her grip and hide her muscles. My sister would show her how to apply makeup and advise her about clothes to restrain the swellings of her muscles. At night though, when the rest of our family was asleep, I'd sneak into my daughter's room and show her what kind of grasp to make in order to scale the bony structure of a high-rise looming over the Chicago skyline.

Sometimes I think about Zephyr the Great's fiancé and the plans they had made, thwarted. I hope some of her ache has begun to subside.

After I have practiced my smiles in the mirror a few more times, I return to Gerald, who waits patiently at the bar. His eyes are large and green and in them I can see tiny reflections of myself, like the wooden dolls that fit one inside each other. I take him in—the bands running down the sides of his neck, the wideness of his forearms. He stands to pull out my stool, but I do not sit. I remain standing, a head above him. It is now or never. I pick up his wrist and place my palm against his; his fingertips loom over mine the way my sister says they should. It is as if a thousand pounds of steel have rolled off my back. A tiny giggle tumbles out the corner of my mouth and I push back the ends of my hair with my fingertips. "You certainly are cute," he says, and I repeat the phrase over in my mind a hundred times. With each repetition I feel myself becoming tiny, perkier, and brighter. My face flushes, matches my sweater.

Finally, I know who I am supposed to be.

*Photo: Monte Gerlach*

Melissa Fraterrigo has published in a variety of literary journals and anthologies. Her stories have been nominated for the Fountain Award from the Speculative Literature Foundation and for a Pushcart Award. She was awarded the Charles B. Wood Award for Distinguished Writing from the *Carolina Quarterly* in 2001 and in 2000, won the Sam Adams/*Zoetrope:All-Story* Short Fiction Contest. This is her first published book in fiction. *The Longest Pregnancy* was also a finalist for the *Other Voices* Books Contest. A graduate of Bowling Green State University's MFA program in creative writing, she now lives and writes in Evergreen Park, Illinois.